DEATH OF AN OLIGARCH

Alan Mackenzie

A thriller by

Alan Mackenzie

Oligarch – a member of an oligarchy. An oligarchy is a form of power structure in which power rests with a small number of people. These people may or may not be distinguished by one or several characteristics such as nobility, fame, wealth, education, or corporate, religious, political, or military control. Throughout history, oligarchies have often been tyrannical, relying on public obedience or repression to exist. Aristotle pioneered the use of the term as meaning rule by the rich, for which another term commonly used today is plutocracy.

CHAPTER 1 – London 1970's

There was nothing in David Mould's genes which predisposed him to become a killer. It was all down to nurture and circumstance.

David was born the youngest of six. In 1967 and after five girls Evie Mould had finally produced a son and heir for her husband Sid and swore blind that she would never become pregnant again. David grew up in a deprived area of London south of the river where life for most families was difficult and prospects for improvement limited. His father had just turned forty when he was born. He had lost his right arm in an unfortunate accident at the age of seven and thus avoided national service during the war. No one knows precisely what happened but playing with his friends by the railway tracks near his house, he had slipped and fell under the 6 o'clock goods train to Millwall Junction. His friends had dragged him screaming to a nearby house where a neighbour tried desperately to staunch the flow of blood with a makeshift tourniquet. In their haste the right arm, severed just below the elbow by the train's wheels, had been left behind on the tracks. The woman of the house dispatched one of the boys to the corner of the street where, luckily, he found a policeman on duty. The ambulance arrived within five minutes and Sid was taken to the local hospital and miraculously survived despite an enormous loss of blood. In fact, Sid was always a survivor and grew up making the most of his one-armed status. In the eyes of many of his mates he appeared a hero. In reality, the accident gave him a lifelong grudge against the world and made him into a sadist who enjoyed inflicting pain on others.

Sid Mould had married Evie at the end of the war when he was eighteen and she was sixteen. The first fifteen years of their life together were devoted to producing their five girls in quick succession, reckoning that economic prosperity would be guaranteed with a large family. They were lucky that the council provided them with a house in Millwall. Sid was able to turn his hand, well, at least his one good hand, to almost anything. With the help of a prosthetic arm, he was able to drive a battered old Vauxhall van and for many years worked as a delivery man for a local paint factory. The prosthetic arm also came in handy when he had to punish his children or his long-suffering wife Evie – an activity which gave him a perverse pleasure. In this, of course, he was limited. After all he did not want to get a reputation as a wifebeater or a child abuser. Once David grew into a young boy, however, he had the perfect victim. By this time, three of the girls – Elsie, Doris, and Jean – had already married and left home.

In punishing his son Sid could always claim he was nurturing him, teaching him how to be a man. From the age of five David had regular beatings at the hands of his father. Sometimes these were perfunctory – a clip round the years, a slap in the face, a kick up the backside. At other times they were protracted beatings with either a leather strap or, worst of all, the prosthetic arm which left bloody welts on the skin. It was during these attacks that the pain and anger David felt gradually changed into a hatred of his dad and a determination that one day he would get his revenge.

Part of Sid's pleasure in inflicting pain on his son was driven by a deep-seated resentment that he might not be his own flesh and blood. While he had brown hair and the girls had all been blondes like Evie, David was unaccountably ginger haired. This was probably a recessive gene. After all, Sid's own grandfather had been a carrot top. But Sid could not get rid of the suspicion that it might have been the result of an illicit union between Evie and the redhaired Alfie who had been a friend at school, lived on his own two streets away and worked at the local abattoir. Every time the thought occurred to him Sid dismissed it, thinking in his overweening vanity that it was preposterous that Evie could prefer the podgy, laid-back Alfie to his own charisma. As David grew, however, it was clear that his son would be tall while Sid was short, would be amiable while he was irascible, kind while he was mean.

By the time David was ten years old, Sid had made his way up in the paint factory to chief warehouseman. Although the job was not very well paid, Sid got by and was able to supplement the weekly wage with odd jobs on the side – not all of which were legal. One autumn evening, it must have been 1975, Sid came home around seven o'clock and took David aside. He glared at him menacingly and said,

"Davey, my boy, you and me is going to have a little outing tonight so get your boots on and follow me!"

Father and son clambered into the van and drove for ten minutes to the paint factory warehouse. All the workers had by then gone home for the day. The firm had had a delivery that afternoon of a thousand pots of gold paint which was to be used to dip Christmas trees in preparation for the markets in November. Sid reversed the van up to the delivery bay and opened the doors to the warehouse to reveal the gleaming tins of gold paint.

"Now Davey, just stack'em in the back of the van as I pass them to you."

Sid handed over the paint pots two by two to David who piled them up in neat, serried ranks of gold at the back of his dad's van. Once they had reached a hundred Sid stopped and looked at what remained in the warehouse. There were so many still left you could not really see any difference in the volume.

"Well done, son. That'll be a nice little earner at Borough Market next Saturday and you can have an ice cream for all your hard work. But don't you go telling no one about our little adventure! It'll be our secret."

David nodded obediently – mainly because he was in fear of the prosthetic arm. But his eyes also gleamed with resentment that he had been forced to help his dad to do something that he knew was wrong. The paint was duly sold off on the market at five shillings a pot and the theft was never discovered at the warehouse.

Sid was never one to miss an economic opportunity and had a feral ability to turn situations to his advantage. He developed a useful side-line in obtaining scrap metal from various mates of his and selling it to the local scrap yards. His friends would come round of an evening and deliver bits and pieces –

leading off a church roof, iron railings, zinc gutters from a building site, copper wiring et cetera – which he would store in the back garden until he had enough to offload to the dealer.

One day when David was about twelve, Sid discovered that his faithful Vauxhall van had finally expired at the ripe old age of twenty-five. At the same time, he now had a small mountain of scrap metal in the backyard which had to be moved. Round the back of the houses in Millwall in an open area behind the allotments lived a group of about fifty gypsies – Sid called them "pikeys" but they were also known to others as didicoys. From their mingled accents it was never clear whether they were Irish travellers or true Romani's. Sid only knew that for a price they could get you almost anything you wanted.

Sid and David wandered over to the gypsy site where twenty caravans huddled together in a muddy field around a smoking central brazier like some Wild West wagon train. On the periphery of the site was a motley collection of old cars, vans, and motorbikes. Four men in black hats, grey shirts, waistcoats, and jeans stood around in earnest discussion while a fifth stood near the entrance to the site, obviously on guard. From the bottom of the field, they could hear the delighted screams of children playing tag.

"Got any vans, mate? Mine's just packed up."

Sid addressed the florid, overweight 50-year-old leaning against the nearest caravan with a lighted cigarette dangling dangerously from his lower lip.

"Depends what you're after, squire. There's an Austin van over there I can let you have for fifty quid. Looks a bit knackered but it still goes."

The man eased himself languidly away from the caravan and pointed to a garishly pink van parked in the mud three caravans down.

"I wanna be sure it goes alright. D'you mind if I take it for a test run?"

The man's eyes narrowed but Sid's question seemed innocent enough and he recognised a fellow haggler.

"As long as you bring it back in one piece!"

The man handed over the keys with a smile which contained more than a hint of menace.

Sid and Dave climbed into the van and with a crunch of gears drove off the site turning left in the opposite direction to their house – he did not want the pikeys to have any clue where they lived. Ten minutes later after a rather circuitous route they arrived back at the house and loaded the scrap metal from the garden. Half an hour later they arrived at the dealers they knew in Shoreditch and managed to get a hundred quid for the lot.

It was a full two hours before they arrived back at the gypsy encampment. The florid faced man seemed not to have moved and the cigarette still dangled from his lip. This time, however, he was not so happy.

"Where the bloody hell have you been? You been using it, 'aven't you?"

"Just wanted to be sure it was worth fifty quid." Sid smiled slyly and paused. "The gears are a bit iffy. Y'know, it's not really what I'm looking for."

The man eyeballed him and turned to whistle to his mates round the brazier. Sid knew it was time to beat a more than hasty retreat. He did not want to risk a punch-up with the likes of pikeys. He knew they could inflict material if not fatal damage.

"C'mon, son, time to scarper!"

Sid and Dave ran out of the site and disappeared up the railway cuttings before the gypsies had had time to group a posse after them.

Looking back, it seemed to Dave that his early life was full of such escapades and was amazed that neither of them ever got nicked by the police. It was not that his dad was a hardened criminal. It was just that he regarded the line between legality and crime as a justifiably grey area subject to interpretation.

By the time David was fourteen he was a full six inches taller than his dad and the punishments which Sid used to enjoy meting out became more difficult to administer. David began to argue and fight back. Blazing rows ensued with Evie trying desperately to mediate between them. Sid would use any excuse to begin an argument with his son all the while looking at his ginger hair which burned into his heart. Things came to a head one warm summer evening when Sid accused his son of stealing his cigarettes.

"You nicked my bloody cigarettes, you thieving little toerag!"

"I did no such thing. Search me if you like."

David glared defiantly at his father over the kitchen table. Evie came in and tried to defuse the stand-off.

"Leave the boy alone, Sid. Here, you can have mine. All this fuss about a silly packet of cigarettes."

Evie threw her packet of cigarettes on the table and moved to put the kettle on for a cup of tea. She had infinite faith that tea could solve all the disputes in the world. It was at that point that Sid's fuse finally snapped. He lunged at his son and threw a fist at the side of his face while his prosthetic arm pushed his son. David was caught off balance and fell back against his mother who yelled out.

"Stop it, you two."

But Sid was not to be deterred and moved forward again, his one fist punching the air, his face red with anger. He was going to teach his boy a lesson he would never forget. David was not going to put up with it. The years of abuse he had suffered at the hands of his father had to come to an end. He boiled with rage as he pushed Sid back and then reached into a kitchen drawer behind him to grab something, anything with which to protect himself. His fingers felt the handle of the sharp carving knife they used for the Sunday roast which he pulled out and brandished in his dad's face.

"You think that's going to frighten me, you fucking little bastard!"

It all happened in an instant. As Sid moved towards his son one more time, David thrust the carving knife forcibly under his father's ribs cutting through the lung and the heart, severing the aorta. Not even a Japanese samurai committing seppuku could have made the cut so efficiently and so lethally. Sid stood back rocking slowly on his feet and gasped at his son in wordless surprise before slumping slowly to the ground against the oven. He looked once at the handle of the carving knife protruding from his stomach. His throat gargled with blood which seeped slowly through his lips. He tried to say something, but his last words were unintelligible. Within seconds it was obvious he was dead. Evie let out a scream.

"Oh, my God, Davey, what have you done?"

Evie looked in shock at the body of her husband, the man she had both loved and hated. She sat down at the kitchen table and held her head in her hands. David's face was expressionless. His emotions were a mixture of pity for the man who had been his father and a strange elation that he had exacted a just revenge. His brain tingled with a rush of dopamine, a heady mix of guilt and pleasure.

After all the fighting and shouting the silence in the kitchen was absolute.

"What are we going to do?"

Evie's question was posed in a whisper. She was horrified by what had happened but had no tears for the man whose body lay on the kitchen floor and who had mistreated her and her son for so many years. She was only thankful that the two younger daughters were not at home – they had gone out for the evening to a dance at the local community centre. The issue now was what to do next and how she could protect her only son.

"I suppose we ought to call the police," said David quietly as he sat down next to his mother.

"You'll go to prison." Eve's voice was flat as she calculated her options. After some time, during which neither spoke, she suddenly stood up and picked up the phone.

"You're not going down for this, David. Not for this shitbag."

Alfie took less than five minutes to drive round to the house. He did not question Evie's decision. He had loved her since they were at school together and was prepared to do anything to make her happy. It was by now eight o'clock in the evening. In the kitchen he stood and looked at Sid's body. He had never liked the man and always thought Evie had made a mistake in marrying him.

There was a moment's silence as he took in the murder scene. He then nodded to Evie and got to work. He took a tarpaulin out of the van and with David's help rolled Sid's body in it. There was surprisingly little blood but then he had died instantly. They dragged and half carried the body on the tarpaulin through the house and placed it in the back of the van. No one saw them in the fading light. They returned to the kitchen where Alfie gave Evie a comforting hug.

"Don't worry, love. I'll sort it. We'll just say he disappeared. Wouldn't be out of character, would it?"

That was the last time any of them spoke about the events of that evening. Sid's daughters were initially puzzled at their father's disappearance but were essentially relieved he was no longer there. People from the paint factory came round to enquire where he was but soon hired a replacement. It was the subject of gossip in the local pub for a few weeks but most of Sid's mates were unperturbed. No one went to the police and there was no report of a missing person. Sid had vanished without trace, and nobody mourned. Only Evie, David and Alfie knew what had happened to the body.

If you know what you are doing, an abattoir is a convenient and efficient place for disposing of a human body. The flesh was cut up, diced, and mixed with other beef products while the bones were crushed and ground and added to the fertiliser bags shipped out every week. The remains of Sidney Mould were probably consumed unknowingly within months in a thousand establishments across London as part of a cottage pie or lasagne.

As for David, the sudden removal of his father from his life and the knowledge that it was he who had killed him had a profound effect on the young boy. He grew into a tall, handsome lad who stood out with his shock of ginger hair, but he also became sullen, argumentative, and prone to pick fights. He was intelligent but resented any form of authority and was frequently threatened with exclusion from his school. He saw rich people in central London in their Jaguars and Bentleys while his mother worked her fingers to the bone to afford the rent and provide food on the table. He saw no future for himself since he would always be on the other side of the class divide, one of the many poor and downtrodden. He appeared to be happy only when he retreated to his bedroom to play on his own with the train set his mother had bought him for his twelfth birthday.

By the time David was sixteen and about to leave school with no qualifications, Evie realised she had to do something, or he would end up in a gang, running drugs or committing robberies or burglaries or some such. She took the decision to drag him off to an army recruitment centre. At least he would have a career, earn good money and, perhaps, come to terms with his life. It was a decision that was to have fatal consequences.

CHAPTER 2 – Cambridge 1999

Things might have turned out quite differently if he had not gone to that party at the end of the Michaelmas term. But then God has an addictive habit of playing dice with people's lives.

It was 1999 and Peter Johnson was in his third year studying history at St John's College, Cambridge. The history teacher at his comprehensive school in Leeds had recognised a bright pupil and entered him for the college entrance exams. To the surprise of both the school and of his parents, he had been awarded a scholarship. Two years into his course during which he had exhibited nothing but industry and diligence, he was now fully expected to obtain a first-class degree when it came to finals.

His tall, lanky frame could often be seen striding through the college clutching books under his arm, his thick crop of blond hair unkempt as usual, sporting a tweed jacket he had bought in a charity shop and wearing scuffed brown leather shoes that had seen better days. He played no sports and had few close friends apart from, despite his socialist leanings, the tubby but likeable Jeremy Rawlings who was a Harrovian, a fellow historian and whose father was in the Lords. Aside from the college history society, he belonged to no social groups and rarely visited the JCR bar. When he did, he restricted himself to a half pint of lager and lime. It was not that he was by nature unsociable nor was he unattractive. He had blue eyes and a handsome face and would have turned the heads of many a female undergraduate if he had been so inclined. It was just that he had no time for what he regarded as idle pursuits. Inwardly, though, he also knew that, with the sole exception of Jeremy, he had a deep-seated and irrational resentment against those from more affluent backgrounds who had come up to Cambridge from their various public schools with an air of natural entitlement.

His tutor, Professor Henry Ramsbottom, a blunt fellow Yorkshireman, was aware that David suffered from an inverted snobbery and often counselled him to forget his prejudices and get out more. On that grey Saturday evening at his last tutorial of the Michaelmas term in his third year the professor was even more direct than usual.

"All work and no play, you know, Peter. Your work is excellent and your last essay on the Romanovs was bloody brilliant. But don't forget that history is made by people, and you've got to get to know them."

He paused, sat back in the chair behind his desk, filled his pipe and lit it, letting the acrid smoke from his preferred cheap tobacco rise gently to the vaulted ceiling of his study in First Court which had been built in the early sixteenth century and had absorbed the smoke of a thousand pipes over the years. Peter looked through the lattice window and almost felt the cold of that gloomy November evening. Henry looked at his student intently, stroked his beard and broke the silence.

"Have you thought what you might do after finals?"

"I thought I might do a PhD. Post-communist Russia perhaps. I might apply to go to Moscow university for a term. As you know, I've been taking a Russian course and it seems to me that what's happening under President Yeltsin is just as momentous as the 1917 revolution."

"Well, of course a PhD is possible but if I were you, I'd think long and hard about an academic life. It's not all it's cracked up to be, you know."

Henry chuckled ruefully to himself as he gently tapped his pipe into a full ashtray. He had become a fellow of the college at the relatively young age of thirty but now, aged sixty, he had only managed to publish one book about the Tudors twenty years ago which had had a mixed if not indifferent reception. He had, however, long ago resigned himself to the fact that he would not live up to his early promise of academic brilliance. He was determined that his students should not make the same mistake of simply drifting into the life of academia.

"There are other avenues you could explore. I know there are many firms in the city who would snap you up. Or you could try the civil service, MI5, or MI6."

"I'm not sure I'm cut out to be a city broker or a hedge fund manager or a spy for that matter."

"Well, have a think about it over Christmas and we can have another chat about it in January. Meanwhile, go out and have a drink and let your hair down for once."

As he descended the stone spiral staircase into First Court and crossed the quadrangle through the college, Peter reflected on his future. He knew that decisions would have to be taken soon. He also knew that, fascinated by history though he was, the life of an academic might not be for him. In forty years' time would he really want to be sitting in a stuffy college room tutoring a motley collection of history students, some of whom might well be less than enthusiastic about the subject they were supposed to be studying?

He was crossing the Bridge of Sighs towards his rooms in River Court the other side of the Cam when he heard the noise of running steps below him and a familiar voice calling out.

"Peter! Are you up for a party?"

It was a rather dishevelled Jeremy – red-faced and out of breath.

"The Arts Theatre is just finishing the last night of some Russian play by a group from St Petersburg, would you believe. Something by Chekhov or Gorky, I don't know which. Probably doom laden and boring with lots of meaningful stuff about the Russian soul. Anyway, the point is we don't actually have to watch the play, thank God. Alexei, my friend from Trinity, has invited us to the after-show party if you're game. It's his last bash before he goes back to Russia."

It was past ten o'clock and Peter was about to decline when he thought of Henry's advice. It was, after all, the end of term.

"Give me a moment, Jeremy, to dump the stuff in my rooms and I'll be with you."

Trinity, the wealthiest college in Cambridge, is just fifteen minutes' walk from St

John's. There has long been rivalry between the two colleges although Trinity would regard itself as superior based on the number of prime ministers and Nobel prize winners it has produced. Certainly, in Peter's time it had a larger number of very rich students – the progeny of presidents and prime ministers from around the world and a sprinkling of young royals and other miscellaneous aristocrats. With the recent collapse of the Soviet empire there had also been an increase in the numbers of the new elites from Eastern Europe – the sons and daughters of multimillionaires. Alexei Tikhonovitch was one of them. His father, Sergei, along with many other born-again capitalists in Russia, had made a fortune buying up state enterprises at knock-down prices as the country descended into near bankruptcy. Alexei had benefited from his father's newfound wealth by being educated abroad at Winchester and then obtaining a scholarship to Trinity. Peter had met him before and had no particular dislike for the young man who was both charming and intelligent. Underneath, however, it rankled with him that Alexei's wealth was based on nothing less than what he considered to be the theft of property from the Russian people.

They walked briskly through the cold November night and made their way to Alexei's rooms in Nevile's Court. They could hear the party as soon as they entered the college. They made their way up to the second floor, all of which Alexei appeared to have commandeered. More than fifty people were competing amongst themselves as to who could shout loudest in either Russian or English and champagne and vodka were circulating freely. Alexei gave them both a drunken embrace and raised his voice to be heard.

"Ah, my friends, thank God you have come. There are far too many Russians here. We need you to dilute the mixture. Come, have a drink."

He pressed a glass of Moët et Chandon in their hands and went off to quieten a quarrel which had erupted between two members of the play's cast as to who was the better actor. Jeremy disappeared and Peter was left in a corner of the room wondering why on earth he had agreed to come. He looked around at the guests. A buxom lady of indeterminate age and with peroxide blond hair was holding forth in Russian with two young men who were evidently students and mesmerised into disbelieving silence by either the woman's charisma or, more likely, by her ample bosom. Four Russian men – three middle-aged and bearded and one totally bald and wearing lipstick – were passing round a bottle of vodka on the other side of the room. Another group was sitting on the steps of the stone stairwell nursing several bottles of champagne.

He finished his glass and was about to leave when he caught sight of her leaning against the wall flanked by two muscular men who looked like bouncers from a seedy nightclub. By contrast she appeared ethereally beautiful – part of the scene and yet not really present at all. A slim girl of about twenty she was wearing a long red dress which contrasted with her black hair. He could see the high cheekbones and the contours of her face and the Gioconda-like smile, as though she was looking on the scene with a mixture of amusement and contempt. Peter realised with a shock that in that instant he was nothing less than smitten.

"Who's that girl over there?"

He had grabbed Jeremy who was stumbling by with a bottle of vodka in each hand.

"Oh, that's Irina."

"Irina?"

"Yes, Irina. She's a friend of Alexei's, not that he's really into girls, you know. Can't remember her second name. I think she's here studying English."

"And Tweedledum and Tweedledee?" Peter indicated the two bouncers.

"That's her protection. Her dad's very rich and the Russian government hate him, so she has bodyguards wherever she goes. If I were you, I wouldn't touch her with a bargepole."

Yes, but I'm not you, Jeremy, thought Peter as he took two more glasses of champagne and walked towards her with a smile. As he approached the bodyguards flinched, but he ignored them.

"Are you not drinking?" he said as he proffered her a glass. She returned his smile, took the glass, and looked at him quizzically.

"And why should I not drink? I am Russian, after all and all Russians drink – sometimes, unfortunately, too much." She nodded her head disapprovingly towards the raucous group of actors.

Her voice was a delicious, velvet mezzosoprano, and her English accent was good with just the slightest hint of those deep Russian vowels and liquid L's.

"How'd you get here?" He realised it was an idiotic question as soon as he had uttered it.

"Well, I walked up the stairs, you know, one step at a time. Very tiring, those stone steps."

She laughed at his evident discomfiture while Peter tried to stammer something sensible. He took in her hazel eyes and the slight imperfection of a mole near her lips which made her more attractive in his eyes.

"I meant…, well, you know,"

"Don't worry, I know what you meant. I grew up in the same city as Alexei – St Petersburg – and our families know each other. When Alexei came to Cambridge to study, I decided I would too. I am studying English at one of the language schools. Do you think I speak it good?"

She sipped her champagne and looked up at him smiling with flirtatious expectation. She knew her English was excellent, and she had deliberately used the adjective rather than the adverb simply to mock him.

"Of course, your English is almost perfect."

"You damn me with faint praise, gentle sir!"

Just then the conversation was interrupted by the sound of the college porters on the steps below. They had come to close down the party, the noise of which had reached as far as the Master's Lodge. The loud voice of the head porter, who was used to corralling recalcitrant and drunken students, boomed up the stairwell.

"Now then, Mr Tikhonovitch, sir, the party's over and I must ask all your guests to leave the college premises. Those who are members of the college should return to their rooms."

Cambridge porters are renowned for their ability to strike the perfect, ironic tone between deference to their supposed "betters" and their own absolute authority within the confines of colleges. No one demurred as the party broke up and the guests made their noisy way home. Peter followed Irina down the stairs.

"I'm sorry, I didn't ask your name."

"It's Irina. Irina Ivanovna Goloshina. And yours?"

"Peter, Peter Johnson. I'm doing history at St John's. Look, do you think we could meet up for coffee or a drink sometime. I'd like to see you again."

One of the bouncers moved between them and Irina waved him away with an imperious gesture.

"Of course, that would be nice. I have a card with my phone number."

She took a card out of her handbag and handed it to him.

"Call me any time and leave a message if I'm not there." She paused to smile. "I shall be pleased to meet you again."

From the bottom of the stairs, he watched her exit the college with her bodyguards either side, a red rose between two black truncheons. He felt a sudden sense of loss. It was ridiculous, he told himself. They had hardly exchanged more than a few words. And yet he knew that he had fallen in love – a 'coup de foudre' or bolt of lightning as the French would have it. The electricity he had felt between them convinced him that the feeling was reciprocated.

Just before ten the next morning, he was looking out of the windows of his rooms over the courtyard as the choristers marched two by two in the crisp sunlight through the college to the chapel for the Sunday morning service and decided to phone her. He went to the porter's lodge at the main gate and dialled the number she had given him. It rang several times before it was picked up.

"Good morning. My name is Peter Johnson. Can I speak to Irina?"

"No Irina here." The male voice was gravelly, decidedly unfriendly, and obviously Russian.

"Irina Ivanovna? We met last night. She gave me this number."

"You must have wrong number."

"But she gave me her card."

"You must be mistaken. Goodbye."

With that the line abruptly went dead leaving Peter holding the phone in a state of profound disappointment that bordered on shock. The card just had her name and a phone number. No address. Why on earth would she have given him a number if it were not correct?

He went to Jeremy's rooms and knocked on the door loudly for five minutes before his friend appeared in a dressing gown holding his head with both hands and groaning loudly.

"Jesus Christ, Peter! Do you have to make such a noise? I didn't get in till four o'clock. Had to wake up the bloody porter to open the gate and suffered the usual bollocking. After the party shut down, we went to the actors' hotel. Big mistake. I shall never mix vodka and champagne again."

Peter followed his friend into the sitting room and sat down while Jeremy continued to massage his head in a vain attempt to massage his hangover away.

"Do you know where Irina lives?" Peter asked barely disguising the urgency with which he needed the information.

"Who the hell's Irina?"

"You know, the Russian girl we met last night. The one in the red dress."

"Oh, that Irina." As though Jeremy knew a multiplicity of Irina's.

"Yes, that Irina." Peter was exasperated.

"Have you got an address? I called the number she gave me but all I got was some Russian who said he did not know any Irina. I think he was lying."

"I've no idea. You could try Alexei, but I think he's already gone down for the holidays.

He's probably on his way back to St Petersburg by now."

He went round to Trinity College only to find that Alexei had, indeed, left to fly home and would not be back until January. He spent the next few days trying to find out from the internet at the college library what he could about the Goloshin family, but the information was sparse. Ivan Vladimirovich Goloshin was briefly mentioned in a business magazine as a prominent entrepreneur in St Petersburg but there was nothing about the family let alone a daughter by the name of Irina.

He took the train back to Leeds for the holidays in a state of despondency and spent Christmas and the New Year trying his best to sound cheerful with his mother and father. He passed a few dreary nights in the local pub with old schoolmates and watched the news in a desultory fashion.

The world limped into the next millennium in a state of paranoia that computers would not be able to cope with three zeros in the date and that energy grids would fail, communications would be disrupted, nuclear weapons would be launched automatically, and aircraft would fall out of the sky. There was a frenzy of futile contingency plans from government departments and international organisations to cope with the expected end of the world. In the event, nothing happened. He watched the handover of the Russian state from the drunken bear of Boris Yeltsin to the little known and unimpressive Vladimir Putin and stayed up on New Year's Eve to see the fireworks in Sydney, London, and New York. All was well with the world and yet nothing was.

As he took the train back to Cambridge in January 2000, he could still not forget the girl he had met so briefly. Who was she really and why had she apparently disappeared? He was beginning to think that he might have invented the whole encounter. That the Russian girl with the velvet voice in a red dress had never existed. That he had not fallen in love that Saturday evening. It might have been better had that been so.

CHAPTER 3 – Germany 1987

Major Rory Connolly, Royal Engineers, was worried. It was not his weight, although he knew he had to do something about that if only to keep his wife Dorothy quiet. It was not the impending large-scale NATO Reforger exercise due to take place at the beginning of September and for which the brigadier had made him responsible for the regiment's logistic support. Nor was it the rain which had soaked the whole of northern Germany for the last few weeks, and which would make the exercise vehicle movements difficult if not, at times, impossible. It was not even the endless planning meetings with the bumptious Americans who would be deploying their M1 Abrams tanks and recklessly churning up all the fields from Paderborn to the border with East Germany at Helmstedt. He knew that, whatever happened, the exercise would be a roaring success. It could not afford to be otherwise with the Russians waiting to gloat at any indication of NATO's weakness. No, he was most concerned about the divisional shooting competition at the end of October which, after two years of ignominious defeats, he was determined to win. And he now had a star shooter.

He looked through his office window at Alanbrooke barracks in Paderborn and fiddled pensively with a sheet of paper on which were written the names of the five best shooters in the regiment. The sky was a dark steel grey, and the driving rain was already threatening to flood the parade ground. For a moment he was depressed at the thought that it would be a messy and muddy September. His mood then suddenly brightened, and he picked up the phone to call the RSM.

"Sergeant major?"

"Yes, sir."

"Can you get hold of corporal Mould for me, please, and ask him to come and see me. As soon as possible, if you will, sergeant major."

"Right away, sir."

At first, David Mould had had problems coming straight from school in adapting to army discipline and the chain of command. In the last two years, however, the major had to admit that the young soldier had made progress and had fully deserved his recent promotion. Above all, he was one of the finest shots in the regiment if not the whole third armoured division. The major looked over his recent scores at the firing range. They were consistently between 96 and 99 percent. No one else came remotely close.

Ten minutes after the call to the RSM there was a knock on the door and corporal Mould came in and stood to attention.

"Corporal Mould, sir, reporting as requested." David looked uneasy as though expecting a reprimand.

"Ah, corporal Mould, thank you for coming to see me so promptly. At ease, please. Take a seat, will you?"

David took off his beret, smoothed his ginger hair back and sat down nervously in one of the armchairs the other side of the desk.

"I suppose you're wondering why I wanted to see you."

David nodded. He first tried to think of any recent transgressions he had committed. He vaguely remembered a drinking bout at the weekend but, as far as he was aware, he had not fought with anyone nor insulted the local German population. It had to be worse than that.

"Are you feeling all right, Mould?" The major could not fail to see how pale the young corporal had become.

"Yes, sir. Just a bit tired."

"Well, I want to talk about something important."

David braced himself. He wondered whether it had to do with his friend Hans Fiedler. Did they know what he had been doing? Was the game up?

"Well, Mould, as you know, the divisional shooting competition is taking place in October. I see you have exceptional skills in that department, and I want you to lead the regimental team of three. The regiment hasn't done too well recently, and I'm determined we should win it this year."

"Of course, sir." David breathed a sigh of relief. Thank God, they did not know.

"Good. Then I shall ask you to choose the other two members of your team. I suggest Osborne and Ainslie. They seem to have pretty high scores. We have to get through this exercise first, of course, but we should have a month for training from the end of September."

"Yes, sir. Thank you, sir."

"Well, that will be all, corporal Mould. We'll meet up again at the end of the exercise."

"Sir."

David put his beret back on, saluted and exited the major's office in a significantly more cheerful mood than when he had entered. Even if he did not have the highest regard for his superiors nor for the Army's rigid class system in general, he recognised that it was an honour to be chosen for any regimental team.

He went back to the NCOs mess and told Osborne and Ainslie the good news about the shooting competition. As it was Friday and the Reforger exercise – this year's codename was Certain Strike – was not due to start until the following Monday, they decided to go into town that evening and celebrate. David also had an ulterior motive – he wanted to see Hans.

His friendship with Hans Fiedler had begun shortly after his deployment to Germany two years previously. They had met in a bar near the Sennelager training camp just outside Paderborn. David wanted to improve his German while Hans, a burly, affable Bavarian with long hair and a brilliant smile, spoke excellent English and seemed to enjoy the company of the British squaddies. They also had a common interest in model railways. He told David he worked as a consultant at the local Nixdorf computer firm. He certainly seemed to have plenty of money and was generous in paying for rounds of beer. Over a period of six months the conversations during those long drinking sessions on a Friday evening gradually turned more frequently to politics.

"Do you really know why you are here, David?" Hans had asked late one evening.

"Of course, we are here to defend Western democracy. Who knows what those bloody Russians might do. At any moment they could roll in the tanks like they did in Czechoslovakia in 1968. And then where would you be, mate?"

David had never been involved in politics. Back in Millwall it had been difficult enough for his mother just to earn a living once Sid had died. Although Alfie helped her out from time to time and David sent money back every month, she still had two jobs cleaning and taking in laundry. As far as he was concerned there was no difference between Conservative, Liberal Democrats or Labour politicians – none of them really cared about the working class. What was the point in getting fussed about politics? It had always been the same for people like him at the bottom of the food chain and nothing would change. In any case he was now a soldier and had to take orders. It was not for him to ask questions.

"So, you think capitalism is better than socialism?" asked Hans as he set down two more beers with schnapps chasers. The bar was due to close and had nearly emptied. They sat alone at a table. The manager was cleaning glasses and looked at them from time to time but was content to leave them in peace. The more they drank, the more money he made.

"Not sure there's much difference."

Hans looked at David intently, took a swig of his beer followed by the shot of schnapps.

"I was born in Bavaria, but all my relatives still live in the Democratic Republic. The other Germany. Just outside Dresden. Do you know they have free education, free housing, and free medical support? They are very happy. The socialist regime looks after everyone. Seems to me that's better than capitalism where everything depends on how much money you have."

By now David was feeling distinctly woozy and had difficulties concentrating but he had to concede Hans had a point. He thought about his mother and how she struggled to make ends meet. It was unfair but that was how life was.

"That's the system, Hans. There's nothing we can do to change it."

"Ah, my friend, there you may be wrong. Things can always be changed if you want it badly enough."

Thereafter, their long late evening conversations often turned to politics. Hans told David how his father had been displaced at the end of the Second World War and had finally settled in Munich where he married and started a family. A second son, his only sibling, had died in a traffic accident. Most of his relations, uncles, aunts, and cousins, however, had remained in the small village of Wilschdorf to the north of Dresden. Hans had taken a physics degree at Munich University and then specialised in computer science before taking the job at Nixdorf in Paderborn.

Most of this was untrue, of course. He did have family in East Germany where he was born but he had no brother, had never studied physics nor computer science, and did not even work at Nixdorf. However, Hans was a professional and had memorised his invented background meticulously and no one, least of all corporal Mould, could ever have suspected that he was an agent of the KGB.

Six months after their friendship began, Hans would often speak about the virtues of the socialist state while inserting into the conversation seemingly idle questions to David about the locations of regiments, the numbers of troops, tanks and transporters, the planning of exercises. By then David had been promoted and moved to the regimental planning staff. His work was just administrative, and he had limited access to the highest classified information, but Hans reckoned that whatever he got out of him might be useful to the KGB in East Germany or even to Moscow Centre. On the other hand, David thought nothing of answering his friend's questions. Most of the information was in any event already in the public domain. It was not until a year before the 1987 Reforger exercise that the penny finally dropped.

"Why do you want all this information? Anyone would think you were a spy." asked

David with a laugh one late summer evening as they were walking to the bar in Sennelager.

Hans stopped and looked directly at his friend without speaking. There was a pregnant pause while David processed the unspoken answer.

"Jesus Christ, Hans! You bloody are." He looked at his friend in disbelief.

"Spy is such an old-fashioned term. I simply transmit information, most of which you can read in the newspapers."

"Transmit? Transmit to who?"

"To those that want to know. To those over the border in the east."

"Bloody hell!" Suddenly the enormity of what David had been doing dawned on him. He had been passing information and, potentially, secrets to the enemy. If he were found out he would be in big trouble. He would be cashiered from the army for divulging secrets to the enemy. Not only a dishonourable discharge but a considerable term in prison.

"Don't worry, David. I won't say a word. And, as I say, most of what you have given me could be found out from reading the newspapers."

David could not suppress a sense of betrayal as he resumed walking to the bar. He had been deceived by his friend, but he also realised that he could not expose him without implicating himself. He had also begun to question himself. Why were they in Germany preparing for war against people who, according to Hans, only wanted to live in peace? Why was life back home so unfair to people like him and his mother while, again according to Hans, the East Germans and Russians lived in a utopia of equality and dignity?

Hans was nothing if not persuasive. David genuinely liked him and began to believe everything he was saying. He convinced himself that giving him the information he requested was in the just cause of solidarity with the working class. He began to pass on copies of classified documents and plans. It all seemed so easy since there were no security checks as he walked out of the barracks and any misgivings that he might have had were dissipated by the warmth of his friendship with the bluff Bavarian.

"You are my friend, David," Hans would say repeatedly. "Friends support each other. What you have done is what any other good man would have done. We are all part of a larger struggle for a better world. But if you have any problems, you have my number and you can call me anytime, day or night. And if you ever want to see what life is like on the other side, you have only to say. I can make the arrangements."

David was remembering these words as he walked to the bar with Osborne and Ainslie that Friday night before the exercise. All three were Londoners, had joined the army at the same time and had remained firm friends since their initial training. The ginger haired David, at six foot three, towered above his two companions. Ainslie, a short, stocky, blond haired ex-boxer with a ripe south London accent peppered with swear words, was the joker of the trio while the more reflective

Osborne, who had inherited his Indian mother's black hair, hailed from Finsbury Park north of the river and was often the butt of jokes from the other two which he suffered with cheerful equanimity. Despite the differences in appearance, they enjoyed each other's company. They also had one thing in common. They were all excellent shots.

The three ordered beers and schnapps and settled in for an evening's drinking. It was the last they would have before the end of the exercise in three weeks. Hans appeared at around ten o'clock and joined the group. David was pleased to see him. The beer and schnapps flowed freely with many declarations from Hans of affection for his "englische Freunde." By midnight they were all singing "Ein Prosit" and "Auld Lang Syne" with their customary drunken gusto. It was to be the last time they would drink together.

CHAPTER 4 – St Petersburg 2001

It was early morning at the beginning of February. Ivan Vladimirovich Goloshin sat in a fur coat and hat on the rooftop of his luxury villa overlooking the Gulf of Finland to the north of St Petersburg and sipped a glass of vodka. As the sun rose and glinted on the waves of the bay of the Neva it could have been a beautiful summer day but for the bitterly cold wind which blew in from the north over the taiga lowlands and mixed with the salty tang of the sea. He could have chosen to stay in his penthouse flat in the city, but he preferred it here where it was quiet in winter. It was also less dangerous.

He rang a bell on the table beside his lounger to call his butler and ordered an espresso and another vodka. He knew he should cut down on his drinking, but it was now the only thing that dulled his sense of impending catastrophe. Life in England had been so ordered, so cultivated, so civilised and he resented having to come back to Mother Russia to protect his interests.

Since his return from London before Christmas 1999, he had spent most of his time playing the stock markets, selling off his shares in vulnerable companies, moving money abroad and, in general, trying to resist the increasing intrusion of the Kremlin into his business affairs. He now realised it was too late. Friends had been arrested on trumped up tax fraud charges. Some had gone to prison. Some had committed suicide and others had simply disappeared.

He always knew things would change under the new president. Just how much was confirmed in July 2000 when Putin summoned the richest men in Russia to a meeting in the Kremlin and told them they would no longer enjoy the special privileges they had had under Yeltsin. The sharks of the Russian economy who had gobbled up state industries in a feeding frenzy were now to be trapped in Kremlin's net. They could keep their money but would not be allowed to interfere with politics. News of the meeting was rapidly leaked, and Ivan knew that the writing was on the wall. Although he was relatively low in the ranking of oligarchs, a minnow compared to other fabulously wealthy Russians, he was still rich, and it was only a question of time before the FSB turned their attention to him.

The threat had been made evident when he received a letter from the President's office at the beginning of December announcing meetings in the New Year of what were ironically entitled "patriotic leaders of Russian industry". No date had been given and he had now been waiting over a month for the call from Moscow.

He took his mobile phone and dialled a number. The call was picked up immediately.

"Sergei? It's Ivan Vladimirovich. Have you had any news about the meeting?"

Sergei Tikhonovitch was his oldest friend with whom he had played as a child in the ruins of what was once Leningrad. They were both born in 1950 and he still remembered how at the age of six or seven they had clambered together over the dusty rubble of the city re-enacting the heroic struggle of the Soviet forces against the Nazis during the Great Patriotic War.

The two friends both studied law at Moscow university and had returned together to their home, now with the restored name of St Petersburg, upon the collapse of the Soviet Union. In the early 1990s they had set up numerous businesses both separately and together and had made money. Lots of money. Most of it had been legitimate; bartering, buying, and selling commodities and shares and taking advantage of St Petersburg's pre-eminence as a trading port for the new Russia. He recognised, however, that some deals had been dubious, particularly those undertaken at the behest of the deputy mayor Vladimir Putin but then everyone was on the make during those chaotic years. Ivan had known what it was like to grow up starving on the streets of a war-ravaged city where only the laws of the jungle applied. Making money was the only way out and it had always been survival of the fittest.

"You've seen the newspapers, I suppose?" replied Sergei resignedly. "There were two gang murders last week in the city and three the week before. These days it's difficult to tell a mafioso from a businessman. The Kremlin is now bound to clamp down on all business but we're still waiting to hear when the president will call this meeting of the so-called leaders of industry."

"Whatever happens, it won't be good news for us, Sergei. Putin will take his pound of flesh. I'm just glad I've paid all my taxes and managed to move most of my money out of the country."

"I'm not sure that will necessarily protect you, my friend. That little bastard is ex-KGB, and they have ways, as you know. You've heard, by the way, that Berezovsky is selling shares to Abramovich?"

"I'm not surprised. Berezovsky's star is waning. He's spent too much time criticizing Putin. I'm also planning to sell the rest of my shares in Russian companies and move permanently to London." He sighed despondently and downed his vodka.

"It's come to something when you're not even welcome in your own motherland."

"Then I would do it as soon as you can, Ivan Vladimirovich. Two more of our friends have already been arrested on charges of tax evasion. Trumped up by the Kremlin, of course but the courts will be directed to convict and who knows what'll happen to them. Siberia for ten years, I shouldn't wonder. Look out for yourself, my friend."

Ivan ended the call in an even greater state of depression. After the unbridled capitalism of the Yeltsin years and the near bankruptcy of the state, he knew that Russia was already changing with the new president. The barbarians were now not just at the gates, they were in the Kremlin.

From the patio of his flat on the tenth floor he could see the city laid out before him – the golden domes of the Saint Isaac's and Naval Academy cathedrals, the Peter and Paul Fortress, the Winter Palace and the canals which fed into the river Neva. He wondered that Peter the Great could have constructed such a thing of beauty on the backs of tens of thousands of serfs who had died building it and whose bodies still lay rotting beneath its foundations. This city, the city of his birth, however beautiful, was still the invention of an autocrat with absolute power. It was a system to which Russia seemed fated always to revert. From Ivan the Terrible through Boris Godunov, Peter the Great and Catherine to Lenin, Stalin and Gorbachev, the country seemed destined to lurch continually between the two poles of anarchy and civil war on the one hand and autocracy on the other. Mother Russia seemed incapable of achieving a stable democracy. Ivan doubted the vicious cycle would ever change and after dabbling with a flawed democracy the country was now due a new dictator.

He got up from the lounger and walked back into the flat through the French doors into a large living room where a log fire was burning. It was now eleven o'clock and he had time to enjoy a late breakfast with his daughter before he was due to chair the management committee of one of his textile companies at three. The maid, Olga, bustled in and took his coat and hat and announced that breakfast had been laid out in the dining room.

"Do you know whether Miss Irina is able to grace us with her presence this morning?" He said this with a smile. His daughter was notorious for sleeping in.

"I'll see whether she is up, sir."

He went into the dining room, sat down, and poured himself yet another cup of coffee. He knew he was perhaps too indulgent towards his daughter but since the death of his wife,

Natasha, from a heart attack five years previously, she had become the centre of his world and he would do anything to protect her. He regretted having had to withdraw her from her studies in Cambridge but, however much he trusted his bodyguards Boris and Yuri, he wanted her nearby in case anything happened.

"Good morning, papa! Sorry to be so late." Irina Ivanovna ran in giggling and gave her father an affectionate peck on the cheek. "I was on the phone with New York till three in the morning with Anna Vassilievna. You remember her? We were at school together. She's just got an internship with some bank or other. Can't remember the name. She's probably laundering your money even as we speak."

Dressed in a red and blue kimono with her long black hair yet to be combed she gave him a radiant grin and Ivan was struck by how beautiful his daughter was and how much she reminded him of her mother at the same age of twenty.

"Irina, we need to talk."

"Oh, papa, don't look so serious!" She was speaking through a mouthful of croissant. "Just tell me we're going back to England. It's been over a year now. St Petersburg is so boring, and all my friends are abroad."

She looked at her father inquiringly and thought how handsome he was with his tall, athletic figure and silver hair. She knew he was very rich and successful, but she was also aware that, even after five years, he was still grieving for the wife he had lost. He had never indicated any desire to remarry, and nothing had come of the few and short-lived relationships he had had over the intervening years. She loved her father and would have done anything to make him happy but just now she could not disguise her frustration at being cooped up in St Petersburg.

"Yes, we are going back to England," said Ivan eventually. "And you can go back to college if you like. Be patient for a few more days. I just have some things to tie up here first and I'm waiting a call for a meeting in Moscow."

"Ah, a meeting with our illustrious new president, Vladimir Vladimirovich?"

"Yes, with the new president." He said this with as much enthusiasm as a convicted man going to the gallows. He was not looking forward to the meeting. There was history between him and the new leader.

They had both grown up in rundown communal apartment buildings in what was then Leningrad where up to five families would share the same kitchen, and hot water and bathtubs would have been luxuries. Ivan was two years older than Putin, but they had attended the same schools – school number 193 and then secondary school number 281. Ivan remembered little of him at the time other than of a diminutive, unremarkable pupil who tended to be withdrawn and taciturn when he was not fighting in the playground. While Ivan was often the soul of the party, Volodya, as Vladimir Putin was known, seemed to have few friends. It did not surprise Ivan, therefore, that while he went on to study law, Volodya joined the KGB. He was surprised, however, to learn in 1994 that he had become first deputy mayor of St Petersburg and chairman of the committee of foreign economic affairs, a post which gave him enormous power in the award of contracts. By this time Ivan was already a successful businessman and had submitted tenders for several contracts. Putin had asked to meet with him and suggested that he should make his tenders more palatable by adding what he called "donations" to the city's finances – another euphemism for the time-honoured tradition of Russian bribery known as blat. Ivan refused. He had finally had enough of the petty corruption that infected every aspect of business.

Needless to say, he was not awarded any of the contracts and had earned the enduring dislike of someone who, against all forecasts, had now become his president. He also doubted that his reputation was very high with the authorities given the funding he had provided to various democracy activists and television networks critical of the regime. He had also contributed articles to various publications including Kommersant and Novaya Gazeta, commenting on the corruption of officials in both St Petersburg and Moscow. Unlike other richer businessmen, he knew he had no godfather in the regime who might protect him from any comeback. He had no "krysha" – the Russian word for roof, that spider's web of patrons, out of sight and unknowable, who could shield you from the envy and revenge of both competitors and politicians alike.

"My dear daughter, I fear it will not be the friendliest of interviews." said Ivan with a sigh. "I suggest you get ready to fly back to England at a moment's notice."

As if on cue, his phone rang. It was the Kremlin inviting him to a meeting with the president the next day.

Ivan took his private jet from Pulkovo airport the next morning at eight o'clock and landed two hours later at Myachkovo airport, Moscow. His car, a black Bentley which he kept at the airport, was waiting for him. The traffic was bad that Wednesday morning and it took more than an hour before he saw the imposing red walls and the golden cathedral cupolas of the Kremlin looming before him. He passed two controls where he was frisked assiduously by security and was eventually escorted by two soldiers into Saint Catherine's Hall where he was asked to wait.

He wondered at the choice of meeting place rather than the president's offices. There was nowhere to sit and no one else arrived and so he wandered alone around the hall under the watchful gaze of the guards. He admired the reliefs on the walls decorated with rhinestones and listened to the echo of his footsteps on the parquet of this grand hall which had been used since the eighteenth century, first as a throne room for Russian empresses and subsequently for meetings of the Soviet of the Union and the Soviet of Nationalities. If he was meant to be intimidated by the grandeur of the scene, to be reminded of how insignificant he was compared to the apparatus of the Russian state, it succeeded.

After forty minutes the doors at the end of the hall were finally opened by two more guards and Vladimir Vladimirovich Putin made what seemed to Ivan to be an unnecessarily dramatic entrance. He cut such a small figure in this huge space as he strutted towards Ivan and yet he carried with him the aura of the most powerful person in Russia.

"Ivan Vladimirovich! It has been a long time." The president shook his hand and gave him what appeared to be a friendly smile although his pale blue eyes were just cold steel betraying no emotion.

"Mr President." Ivan could not bring himself to address him with the familiar name Volodya and he even felt an irrational urge to bow or even to kiss the ring as though this man standing before him in the hallowed hall of the Russian empire was, indeed, a reincarnation of Peter the Great. Here was a man who would be the new tsar.

"Let us take a walk." The president began mooching pensively around the hall his hands behind his back and Ivan could do nothing but follow.

"I was sorry to hear about the death of your wife. I understand your daughter, Irina, still lives with you?"

"Yes, she does, Mr President."

"You have done well since we were at school in St Petersburg." Where was this conversation going, Ivan asked himself.

"I am informed that you are now one of the most successful businessmen in Russia and are now worth more than 950 million dollars?"

The figure, although exaggerated, indicated that the president had been well briefed and wanted Ivan to know that he knew all about his family and businesses.

"My predecessor, Boris Nikolayevich, presided over some difficult times for our country, as you know, but I want you to understand that things will now be different under my presidency. Russia will be great again."

Ivan said nothing but continued to follow the president's aimless perambulation around the hall like a faithful family dog following his master. Putin pointed out the various paintings and reliefs and spoke admiringly about the meetings that had been held there under Stalin, Khrushchev, and Brezhnev when the USSR had been a power in the world to be reckoned with.

"That time will come again, Ivan Vladimirovich." Putin had suddenly stopped and turned to look up at Ivan who was at least half a foot taller. He spoke so softly that Ivan had difficulty hearing and had to bend his head towards him. There was no doubt, however, as to the underlying menace in his voice.

"I want you to know that I expect you and the others who have profited so much under my predecessor, to contribute to this process. I am sure you will have no objections to coming to the aid of our beloved mother Russia?"

Putin's thin smirk as he said this indicated that his question was really an instruction. The tsar was giving an order to his subject. Ivan nodded. What could he say? He was increasingly confused at this surreal interview. Where were the others? The other oligarchs who had siphoned off billions from former state industries. And was this conversation being recorded or filmed? He could not see any cameras, but this did not mean they were not under surveillance by the FSB, the Federal Security Service which had succeeded the KGB, the Committee for State Security.

"Don't worry, I shall be speaking to the others, Ivan Vladimirovich." The president turned away indicating the end of the interview and then stopped and looked at Ivan.

"By the way, I suggest you don't write any more newspaper articles. They're not very good, you know. The guards will escort you out."

With that the president abruptly ended the conversation and swaggered back out of the hall while two guards indicated that Ivan should follow them to the exit.

In the car on the way back to the airport Ivan reflected on the meeting. What had been the point of dragging him all the way from St Petersburg to tell him no more than could have been communicated in a telephone call? Then he realised it was simply an exercise of power. Putin wanted to show that he could summon anyone from anywhere and at any time.

Back in St Petersburg Ivan immediately prepared to return to London. His meeting with the president had reinforced his suspicion that everything he had – position, power, money, even his life – was under threat. What the president had hinted at concerning so-called contributions was merely the beginning. They would come after him, he was sure. Just five days after his return a call one evening from his principal lawyer, Ilya Mikhailovich, confirmed that the screws were tightening.

"Ivan Vladimirovich, we have a problem."

"What kind of problem?"

"I have just received a demand from the tax authorities which you will not believe."

"A demand? Surely, we have paid in full all our taxes?"

"We have but they claim the amount is insufficient and that you owe a further three hundred million dollars."

Ivan drew a breath. It was a ridiculous amount which risked bringing him to the brink of bankruptcy. He might be considered rich but most of his wealth was tied up in fixed assets and shares which would take time to liquidate.

"There must be some mistake."

"We can appeal, of course, but the likelihood of success in the current climate is minimal at best."

Ivan thought quickly. He could find the money eventually, if necessary, but this was unashamedly state extortion. So, this was what Putin meant by contributing to Mother Russia.

"The situation is worse, I'm afraid," his lawyer paused.

"I can't imagine it being much worse."

"It can. You are being charged with tax evasion, Ivan Vladimirovich, and I understand that a warrant for your arrest is about to be issued. The penalty is up to ten years in prison or even hard labour in a penal colony. I'm here to help you at any time, my friend, but I would advise you now to consider all options. You know what I mean. I'm not sure how much time you have."

As Ivan put the phone down, he recalled what his friend Sergei had told him and realised that he himself was now at risk of being sent to Siberia. It was only a question of time and that was now limited. Ilya had talked of options but in reality, he only had one.

He called Irina in, explained the situation, and told her to pack immediately. He summoned his bodyguards Boris and Yuri, instructed them to make the necessary arrangements for his private jet and then told Olga that they were going away for an unspecified time. He did not tell her the destination. The less she knew the better. By midnight, less than four hours after the call with his lawyer, they had taken off from Pulkovo and were on their way to London.

The next day at eight o'clock the FSB raided the offices of his companies in both St Petersburg and Moscow, sent the staff home and impounded documents and computers. His accounts with Bank Rossiya were frozen and trading in the shares of his enterprises on the St Petersburg Stock Exchange and the Moscow trading system were suspended. At ten o'clock two FSB officers turned up at his flat in St Petersburg with a warrant for his arrest on charges of tax evasion. Olga could tell them nothing about his whereabouts but could not prevent them from searching the flat. His lawyer, Ilya Mikhailovich, was detained later that afternoon but released once it was clear he knew nothing about his client's location. It did not take long, of course, before the authorities found out that his jet had flown to London. By then it was too late. Ivan Vladimirovich Goloshin had evaded arrest but was now persona non grata in Russia and effectively an enemy of the state.

CHAPTER 5 – Germany 1987

Preparations for the exercise began precisely at midnight on Saturday. Hundreds of tank transporters began moving from barracks across northern Germany and snaked their way in the dark through the pouring rain like gigantic mechanical slugs towards the assembly areas between Hildesheim and Helmstedt. They were accompanied by innumerable numbers of troop and gun carriers, fuel lorries and jeeps. The routes had been planned in meticulous detail to avoid any gridlocks. The motorways and access roads sparkled with red and amber lights and hummed with the sound of engines. Exercise marshals, medics, German police, damage control units, engineers, logistics and staff officers scurried along the traffic lines in their jeeps shepherding their charges towards their designated rallying points. There were Leopard tanks from German units, Chieftains from the British and M1 Abrams from the US. As a weak sun rose hesitantly towards morning and the rain abated for the first time in weeks, the transporters disgorged these mighty engines of war onto sugar beet and rape seed fields and troops began to set up mess tents, latrines and communications and medical posts. To an outsider it might have seemed chaotic but in fact everyone knew where they were going and what they had to do.

It took five days before everything was in position and the exercise proper started. This was when the generals arrived to exercise command and control. A virtual inner German border had been established fifty kilometres west of the real one behind which units of the Allied forces designated as the "enemy" arrayed themselves for the imaginary invasion. Major Rory Connolly was pleased at the way the regiment had conducted themselves in this preparatory phase and reported as such to the brigadier that evening.

"Everything's in position, sir. Fortunately, despite this bloody weather, there have been no major snarl ups."

"Jolly good, major. General Fanshawe is due to arrive in about half an hour and we'll have a staff meeting at eight o'clock Zulu. Pass on my thanks, will you, to the platoon commanders for all the efforts they've made."

Major Connolly began walking back in the dark towards the mess tent looking forward to a strong cup of tea with a nip of whiskey. He cursed to himself as a cold drizzle began falling again. Just then he heard a shout and he turned to see corporal Mould running across the soggy field towards him.

"Major Connolly, sir. We have a problem."

"Well, what is it, Mould? Spit it out!" He was irritated. Everything had been going so well and now his evening was about to be ruined.

"I've just come from HQ, sir. There's been an accident with a tank. Someone's been injured. The medics are there but they want a staff officer to decide what to do. Happened about two miles down the road."

They commandeered a jeep and sped towards the accident. As they drew near, they could see a Chieftain tank at the edge of a field tilted at an unusual angle and surrounded by lights, medics, and the German and military police. As they stepped out of the vehicle, they could hear the soft moaning of a man trapped under the tracks. A medic explained what had happened.

"The ground just gave way, sir. Not surprising what with all this rain. Corporal Ainslie is trapped with both legs under the left track. They're clearly broken and he's losing blood. We've given him morphine but he's in a bad way, I'm afraid."

"How the hell did he get himself in this position in the first place?" asked the major irritably.

"Dunno, sir. Trouble is, we need to do something soon."

Corporal Mould knelt beside his friend and began speaking to him but there was no answer, just a shallow breathing and a continuous, pitiful moan.

Major Connolly reflected on what to do. There were limited options. A Chieftain tank weighed more than fifty tons. It would be impossible to dig the man out without risking a complete collapse of the earth bank. They could arrange to lift the tank up on its side, but this would take time which they did not have and would in any event add to the man's injuries. There was only one thing to do, however risky it might be. He instructed the tank crew to start the tank up and put it in reverse.

"You do realise, sir, that this could kill him?" asked the medic.

"Of course, I know that." replied the major bitterly. "We've no fucking choice."

The Chieftain's 750 horsepower engine roared into life and, with smoke belching, juddered loudly into reverse spraying mud and earth all around. It hesitated for a fraction of a second then moved quickly backwards, the tracks digging deeply into the ground. The man left on the ground uttered one piercing scream and then fell silent. The medics rushed over but there was nothing to be done. Both legs had been crushed to a pulp and he had lost too much blood. As the Chieftain's motor cut out there was a palpable silence in the crowd surrounding corporal Ainslie's lifeless body.

"Stupid accident." mused Major Connolly as he wondered how to explain this to the brigadier.

Corporal Mould stood rooted to the ground in shock as the medics took Ainslie's body away. This had been his friend. Someone he had known ever since they joined the army. They had trained, laughed, and got drunk together and now his life had been snuffed out in a pointless accident. Not for the first time he considered why he was there and then he thought of what Hans had been telling him repeatedly – how the West was corrupt, how capitalism had no future, how he was fighting for the wrong cause, how socialism would triumph in the end. With a start he realised what he must do.

He excused himself from the major and walked back to the tent he was sharing with three others. He told them about the horrific accident and the death of his friend. He put on his trench coat and told them he was going for a short walk. They understood he needed some time for himself. They little suspected his real intentions.

It was just seven o'clock in the evening and reveille was not until five the next morning, so he had plenty of time. He set off at a brisk pace down the country road covered in mud from the tanks, jeeps and lorries which were feeding the exercise preparation. Army vehicles passed him by, lights glaring through the drizzle laden darkness, and the sweet stench of fuel mingled with the fresh rain. No one stopped to ask where he was headed. They assumed he was on some mission or other.

After about an hour he left the noises of the exercise behind and came to a crossroads with the main Landstrasse to the east. He crossed this and took another small country road which brought him half an hour later to the small village of Steinbruck. The rain had eased off although the damp air still chilled him to the bone. The only light in the village was provided by the local Gaststätte 'Zum Blauen Ritter.' As he entered the bar the three elderly men sitting by the log fire drinking their beers looked at him with curiosity and grunted a good evening. If the landlord was surprised to see a lone British soldier order a beer on a Sunday evening during what he knew was the exercise season, he showed no sign. David took a grateful draught of his drink and asked to use the telephone. After the briefest of conversations, he then sat down at a table to wait.

Hans did not arrive until eleven o'clock by which time the bar had emptied and the landlord was impatient to close. With great reluctance he acceded to Hans' request for two more beers and schnapps making it clear that he would be shutting up shop in ten minutes.

"Sorry to be so late, my friend." He spoke quietly in English. He did not want the landlord to overhear the conversation. "A lot of traffic on the road. Too many bloody tanks, you know?" Hans sat down at David's table, smiled, and lifted his glass in salutation. He then looked at his friend intently and then began whispering conspiratorially to make sure the landlord could not hear.

"You realise, David, that this is a one-way journey. An Einwegstrasse you could say. No turning back. There can be no regrets, no second thoughts. Are you prepared?"

"I know. I've thought about it a lot. It's what I want to do."

"Very well, then. I have a change of clothes for you in the car and a new passport. You are now Martin Hauptmann. It will take about an hour to the border and then you will begin your new life In the German Democratic Republic."

They arrived at the border crossing of Helmstedt-Marienborn just after midnight. The West German guards waved them through after a perfunctory check of their passports. It was the night shift after all, and they were more concerned about people coming into the West rather than those poor deluded souls going the other way. At the second checkpoint the Soviet and East German guards initially eyed them both suspiciously and took some time to peruse their documentation. After ten minutes David began to feel nervous. Were they about to be arrested? Finally, Hans lost patience, spoke to the Soviet guard in fluent Russian and showed him a separate ID. They were immediately let through the crossing with many apologies for the delay.

They drove on in silence into the darkness, each lost in their own thoughts. Hans anticipated how he would be congratulated by his superiors in Dresden on recruiting to the cause a British soldier no less. This would surely be a coup worthy of promotion. David, meanwhile, was trying to process the reality of the decision he had just made. He looked at the passport that Hans had given him. His name was now Martin Hauptmann and although his birthday was the same, he had apparently been born in Dresden. With a shock he realised he had turned his back on the army and his family, betrayed his country and was now facing a new existence in a culture and a people about which he knew very little. It was a daunting prospect but at the same time he felt a sense of exhilaration. He had crossed a line into the unknown and it was now up to him to make his new life work.

****

David's disappearance was not discovered until Monday morning's rollcall. The RSM reported it to Major Connolly shortly after five o'clock before the staff meeting at six.

"What do you mean, he's disappeared?"

"He went out last night, sir, just after the accident and never came back."

"Where the fuck is he?" Major Connolly could feel his blood pressure rising. One of his soldiers disappearing on exercise was the last thing he wanted after the unfortunate death of corporal Ainslie.

"We've got the German and military police out searching for him, of course. Could be he just got lost, sir. I'll let you know immediately if we have any news."

"Jesus Christ, sergeant major! Anyone would think this exercise is jinxed. And of all people, corporal Mould. I was relying on him for the divisional shooting competition."

Major Connolly reported the events of the night to the staff meeting and met alone immediately after with the brigadier. He knew he would have to carry the can even if he was not directly at fault. One month after the exercise he was transferred back to the UK to a desk job in the Ministry of Defence. As a final insult, he heard at the end of October that his regiment had lost the annual shooting competition.

Over several months the German and military police extended their search for corporal David Mould to cover the whole of West Germany. Enquiries were even made in Belgium and the Netherlands and a RMP officer turned up one morning on Evie Mould's doorstep in Millwall to ask whether she had heard from her son. She had not, of course, but she promised to let the authorities know if he contacted her while inwardly swearing to herself that she would never do so. Her only son must have his reasons and there was no way she was going to snitch on him.

The months turned into years with no news. David Mould had disappeared off the face of the earth. Officially he was designated as AWOL – absent without leave – such an elegant bureaucratic phrase for a person's disappearance. His case file gradually gathered dust, and no one undertook any further active searches. Strangely, though, no one could conceive of the possibility that he might have defected.

CHAPTER 6 – London 2001

At the beginning of 2000 Peter Johnson took his tutor's advice and armed with a glowing recommendation from his college, applied to join MI5. He was subjected to the usual positive vetting procedures which involved extensive interviews of his parents, his friends and his professors at Cambridge and a final panel at MI5 where three members of the service quizzed him about his personal life, his loyalty to the United Kingdom and his motives and expectations. He had in fact only the vaguest notion of what the work might entail and still had reservations about his career choice by the time he received a letter at the end of October from the head of MI5 congratulating him on his First in his final history exams and offering him a post as an intelligence analyst. He accepted and was directed to report for work in London in the New Year.

In November he rented a small two bedroomed flat above a fish and chip shop in Kilburn together with his friend Jeremy

Rawlings who was to start work at the Home Office at the same time. Together they spent the last weeks of the year enjoying the sights, sounds and taverns of London, considering that this represented the end of their student days and that they would shortly embark upon what their parents ominously designated as "solid careers". On Monday, 8 January 2001 he reported for duty at Thames House, the grandiose edifice of the security services on the north bank of the Thames. He went through security and was welcomed by the personnel services before being introduced to the head of analysis who assigned him to a desk in a three-man office to the rear of the building where the sun rarely shone.

The first few months were devoted to improving his Russian and various induction courses about the role of the security services. Any fanciful notions he might have had about becoming a James Bond character were quickly dispelled. His job entailed monitoring the Russian press, preparing briefings for senior staff and ministers, keeping tabs on persons of Russian nationality in the UK who were of special interest and making sure that MI5 also received any relevant information from GCHQ, MI6 and the Financial Services Authority, the FSA, the importance of which had grown with the number of wealthy Russian oligarchs who had made their home in the capital since the collapse of the Soviet Union. Most of the work was, in fact, rather dull and he met no one who looked even remotely like a character from a John Le Carré novel let alone James Bond.

He was in the office one Thursday afternoon in late August sweltering from an unprecedented heatwave against which the tiny office fan had no effect – the government office services had no money at that moment to install air conditioning. His two colleagues had sensibly taken the afternoon off, and he was left alone. He had finished his daily report on articles of note in the Russian press. The main topic of interest was the tragedy of the sinking of the nuclear-powered submarine, the Kursk, on August 11 with the loss of 118 crew and the apparent insouciance of Putin who remained on holiday at Sochi on the Black Sea. This caused widespread criticism of the regime in addition to the continuing grumbles about the military operations in Chechnya.

He then began to look through the British newspapers. Suddenly he came across an article in the Guardian entitled "The New Tsars." It was a vitriolic denunciation of the Kremlin with allegations of corruption made against almost everyone in the Russian government including the president himself. It was a brave dissident voice from a Russian national abroad, but it was not so much the article that got his notice – such criticism was rife these days. It was the author. Ivan Goloshin, the father of Irina, the girl he had met in Cambridge over a year before. The editor's by-line stated that Goloshin had left Russia and was now living permanently in London seeking political asylum. He was also fighting extradition procedures in the British courts brought against him by the Kremlin on charges that he had deliberately evaded taxes. Did this mean that Irina was also here? Would it be possible somehow to contact her? Or was he just pursuing some adolescent fantasy about being in love?

For some reason Goloshin was not yet on MI5's list of persons of special interest. He rang the Guardian and asked for Goloshin's address or phone number but was told the information was confidential and they could not in any event divulge such information even to such an august body as the MI5 without a court order. Typical of the Guardian, he thought. He tried the central archives in MI5 but was informed that information on Goloshin was limited and that he was in any case not such a "big fish". His contacts in GCHQ and MI6 were similarly unable to give him any clues as to where exactly in London he might live. As he left the office for home it seemed that he would never be able to track down the girl. It was then that God threw the dice once more.

He decided to take Friday off and look for a present for his mother whose birthday was coming up. He would make a surprise visit back home to Leeds, he thought, and give her some expensive perfume. He took the tube down to Knightsbridge. It was another glorious summer day. He entered Harrods and made his way to the perfume department. It was crowded with well-heeled shoppers – women overspending their husbands' allowances on exotic French fragrances from Dior and Chanel and sharp suited businessmen buying for their wives or mistresses. An attentive assistant pressed him into smelling an extremely expensive scent from Roja.

"It has a lovely fragrance, don't you think, sir? Your wife or girlfriend would love it. And we have a special promotion today. Only £400."

It was far too steep for Peter's income, so he moved on to the economy brands. He was about to leave thinking he might find a better deal at John Lewis or Selfridge's when he caught sight of her on the other side of the counter. She looked stunning in an immaculate and obviously expensive red summer dress and a matching Fedora. For a moment he hesitated, unsure as to whether it was really her. But it was the same black hair, hazel eyes, and the same mole near her lips. Would she even remember him? He decided there was nothing to be lost.

"Irina?"

He spoke a little too loudly for one middle-aged woman who looked at him askance, affronted at this sudden and unwelcome intrusion into her shopping spree. Irina looked across the counter in surprise and smiled.

"The young man from Cambridge."

"Yes. Do you remember me? My name is Peter. Peter Johnson."

"Peter Johnson." She looked reflective for a moment and then said impulsively with a laugh, "Well, Mr Peter Johnson. You can come over here and help me decide."

He made his way through the crowd at the counter as she proffered her wrists to him.

"Which do you like best?"

He bent to smell the scents on her wrists, first one and then the other. They were both intoxicating as was the reality that she was standing there in front of him. He looked up quizzically and met her eyes, ignoring the middle-aged woman who was now tut-tutting at this apparent show of intimacy between two young people. Irina laughed and then turned decisively to the shop assistant.

"I think I shall take both."

She paid for her purchases and then suggested that they went for lunch. Outside Harrods she hailed a taxi and announced that they were going to the Ritz. By this time Peter had hardly said a word, breathlessly following her lead and beginning to realise that this young lady was a force of nature.

It was a long lunch at which Irina insisted on buying a bottle of Dom Perignon to celebrate their reunion. Given the fact that they had exchanged only a few words at that Cambridge party, it was strange that they chatted away like old friends. But then Irina was obviously delighted at her tall, handsome Englishman while Peter could not believe his luck in finding her again. She told him how boring it had been in St Petersburg, how her father was under pressure from the current regime in the Kremlin and how pleased she was to be back in England where she was now studying to be a paralegal and hoped to take up a place at King's College London to do law. Peter talked about his parents in Leeds and the success in his exams which he put down to luck rather than academic brilliance and how he had joined MI5 as a Russian analyst.

"Oh, so you're a spy?" Irina giggled the word.

"No, far from it." Then he put a finger to his lips and with a conspiratorial smile whispered in mock confidentiality, "but don't tell anyone."

After lunch they came out onto Piccadilly where Irina looked for a taxi to take a back to the house her father had bought in Hampstead. Peter decided to take the tube.

"Can I see you again?"

"I should like that."

As a taxi arrived, on an impulse he drew her towards him and kissed her. She pressed against him and returned the kiss. It was at that precise moment that each knew they were in love.

The next few weeks passed by in a blur of dates and assignations. They went to art galleries, restaurants, and the theatre. Peter took her to see The Mousetrap which she found so quaintly English but not particularly good. Irina took him to see Boris Godunov at the Royal Opera which he found impressive but gloomy. They delighted in each other's company. She liked his self-deprecating sense of humour while he loved her unpredictability. Sometimes they spoke Russian with Irina teasingly correcting Peter's pronunciation and quoting extracts from Pushkin's Eugene Onegin, parts of which her father had forced her to learn by heart. Peter retaliated with speeches from Henry V and Julius Caesar. They met each other's friends in bars and by the end of November it was evident to all that they were a couple.

"You are my Lensky," she would say affectionately, recalling a character from Eugene Onegin.

"Then you must be my Olga," he would reply laughing and then suddenly realised that Lensky's fate was to be shot dead in a duel with Onegin while defending Olga's honour.

"God, I hope I don't end up like him."

The only mystery was that, while Peter frequently invited her back to his flat in Kilburn, she always declined saying that she had to get back to her father in Hampstead who, despite dispensing with bodyguards for her, still worried about her safety.

One Friday at the beginning of December, however, she accepted his invitation and phoned her father to say that she was staying over with a girlfriend. Jeremy had gone away for the weekend, and they had the place to themselves. They made love for the first time, and it was for both a magical experience which sealed their relationship.

They woke late the morning after. Peter lay in bed observing Irina dress with her back to him, her black hair falling on her shoulders, her perfect body framed in the window through which filtered the winter sun. It occurred to him just how erotic it was to watch a woman dress. Irina was aware of him watching her and turned around slowly as she buttoned her blouse. She came to him, kissed him lightly on the lips then said coquettishly,

"Now that you've taken advantage of me, Peter Johnson, I think it's time you met my father."

He was silent for a moment. She had told him all about her father. How he had made millions in St Petersburg under the Yeltsin regime, how he had become disenchanted with the criminality and corruption in Russia and how his critical newspaper articles had earned him the undying enmity of the Kremlin. Now he was about to meet the man himself.

"Well, I'd better have a hearty breakfast first just in case he decides to shoot me," he said with a wry smile.

It took less than twenty minutes to drive over to Hampstead in Peter's second-hand VW beetle. It stopped outside an imposing house just after eleven. Irina punched in the security code for the gates which opened slowly to let the car in. A cobbled driveway led to a courtyard in front of the house where a thickset, black suited bodyguard stood. Peter recognised him from Cambridge.

"Good morning, Boris Ivanovich. This is my friend, Peter."

"Good morning, Miss Irina."

Boris Ivanovich Kalunin was an imposing figure, six foot six tall and over twenty stone, with thick black hair framing a large, saturnine face and a squashed nose that had been frequently broken in professional boxing fights. He had grown up an orphan in the tenements of St Petersburg and was devoted to Goloshin who had taken him out of the ring and employed him for over ten years.

Boris bowed his head deferentially to the lady of the house and nodded to Peter. As they entered through the front door a maid appeared from nowhere to take their coats. Peter stood still for a moment in the large hallway from which a grand wooden staircase swept up to the first floor. He took in the chandelier hanging from the ceiling and the numerous paintings hanging on the walls. He recognised a Rothko, a Paul Klee, and a Modigliani, all of which seemed originals. The house was a substantial Georgian property and undoubtedly listed, he thought. Vastly different from the semi-detached house of his parents in Leeds. For the first time it came home to him just how rich Irina's father must be.

"We also have a small estate in Hampshire," said Irina, "a place in Spain near Malaga, a flat in New York and a villa just outside Buenos Aires but papa prefers staying in London." She paused and looked at Peter intently, aware of an unspoken criticism.

"I know what you're thinking, Lensky. That we're disgustingly wealthy. You may be right, but papa came from very humble beginnings, you know, and you'll find that all this means little to either him or me." Another pause and then a chuckle. "He just thinks he needs as many escape routes as possible. Come on, he's probably in the library."

She led the way through a warren of hallways to the side of the house and opened the double doors to a magnificent library with books from floor-to-ceiling and French windows which looked over Hampstead Heath. A fire was burning in the large fireplace in front of which stood Ivan Vladimirovich.

"Irina, my darling daughter, where have you been? I was beginning to worry."

"No need to, papa." She took his arm, kissed him on the cheek and turned with a smile to introduce Peter.

"This is my friend, papa. You know, the one I've been telling you about."

"Ah, so this is your Peter." He spoke in Russian, looked him up and down appraisingly and then offered his hand.

"Mr Goloshin, I'm so pleased to meet Irina's father." Peter was conscious that his English sounded insincere, stilted and far too formal.

"You're the spy from MI5?"

For a moment Peter was nonplussed at the aggressive tone. Then Ivan laughed at his discomfiture, a deep Russian growl of a laugh.

"You think I wouldn't do a background check on the sort of people my daughter associates with? Don't worry, Peter. I'm happy if Irina is happy and as long as you're not the FSB. Let's dispense with formalities. You must call me Ivan. I may be living in England in a splendid Georgian house far away from the mother country but at heart I'm still a Russian peasant. We'll have lunch, drink vodka, speak Russian and you can tell me all about yourself."

The lunch lasted a long time and Peter was exhausted by the time he got back to Kilburn at around six in the evening. Irina's father had told him about his difficulties in the British courts fighting extradition by the Russian government and the delays in his asylum request which had been sitting on the Home Secretary's desk for months. Peter decided that, in addition to being passionately in love with Irina, he liked her father. Contrary to the impression given in the British press of most Russian oligarchs, Ivan Vladimirovich seemed much more concerned about the fate of his country and his people than his own obvious wealth. Whether Ivan truly liked Peter, who was bound by the Official Secrets Act to avoid being specific about his work, was, of course, another question.

On the following Monday morning Peter was unexpectedly called in to the office of his department head for what his secretary mysteriously termed "a little chat". James Greenwood, an Oxford graduate barely three years older than Peter himself, was a highflyer destined for great things in the service and renowned for having a straightforward if not blunt management style.

"Do sit down, Peter. This won't take long. I'm told that you have recently become friendly with a certain Ivan Vladimirovich Goloshin."

Peter was taken aback. Was MI5 itself monitoring his movements?

"You shouldn't be too surprised. You'll appreciate that we must make sure that, due to the nature of the work, our own employees are never compromised. You know that Kompromat is a currency easily exchanged."

He paused to let the words hang in the air.

"Don't worry. You're not under suspicion of doing anything illegal nor are you under any direct surveillance. You're perfectly entitled to associate with whoever you like. Within reason, of course. We're still a democracy, after all. Sometimes, however, it is useful for us to have informal feedback on persons of special interest. Goloshin has recently become such a person due to his strong and very public stand against the current regime in the Kremlin."

He paused again and looked straight into Peter's eyes as though debating how to continue.

"I understand you are close friends with his daughter. You're under no obligation but any information you might find out which could be of use to us would be greatly appreciated."

For a moment Peter said nothing, trying to take in the implications of what was being requested.

"You mean act as a spy?"

"I wouldn't put it that way. Think about it."

The conversation ended abruptly, and Peter returned to his office in a state bordering on shock. He had known what MI5 did but spying on friends and acquaintances was not something he had signed up for and, informal or otherwise, there was no way he was going to provide feedback in any way on his relations with the father of the woman he loved. He was beginning to think that perhaps he should have become an academic after all.

CHAPTER 7 – East Germany 1987

It took more than seven hours to make the journey from Helmstedt to Wilschdorf, a small village to the north of Dresden. The old Trabant which Hans was driving could not do more than fifty miles an hour and it even found that exhausting, the engine coughing and spluttering asthmatically with the effort. They had to stop three times to let the motor cool down. Dawn was breaking with the morning sun peering through the mist over the fields as they finally arrived in a farmyard to the sound of cocks crowing and birds singing in the trees. The rain, which had followed them persistently the whole journey, had finally stopped. Despite his exhaustion, David had slept only fitfully but was fast asleep when Hans shook him awake.

"We have arrived, my friend."

"Where are we?" David, still groggy, looked around and took in the scene. All he could see was a collection of solid, grey concrete buildings surrounding a muddy courtyard where two tractors were parked.

"This is my cousin's farm. It is near Dresden. Welcome to the German Democratic Republic. You will stay here for a time. Remember that from now on your name is Martin Hauptmann."

Hans stepped out of the car and led the way over the yard to the front door of the first building. As they approached, it opened and a large, blond-haired, middle-aged woman with a ruddy complexion stood smiling in a voluminous blue dress and wiping her hands on her apron.

"Hans, my dear, how lovely to see you. Come in, come in! But I did not know you were arriving today."

"I telephoned Fritz yesterday, Helga."

"Ah, that Fritz. He tells me nothing and would forget his own name if I did not remind him."

Hans made the introductions and explained that his friend Martin, whom he had met on one of his business trips to Los Angeles, had spent many years in the United States which accounted for his rusty German. His mother and father had recently died and with no other relatives and disillusioned by life in the States, had now decided to return to the land of his birth – his Fatherland. He uttered the word with an ironic grin and clapped David on the shoulder.

"Nicht wahr, mein Freund?

David smiled sheepishly in return but said nothing as they sat down at the large wooden table in the middle of a farmhouse kitchen. Helga busied herself with setting out ham, sausage, cheese, hard boiled eggs, and rye bread for breakfast while keeping up an unending flow of anecdotes about life in the village. How Frau Dönitz had recently broken her leg. How a Russian soldier had almost drowned in the village pond after drinking too much and had to be rescued by Fritz. How life was getting increasingly difficult and expensive largely due to those incompetent politicians in Berlin. Of course, it was the Americans who were really at fault. They just wanted to sow discontent and destroy any socialist state. Before Helga could warm to her theme about the iniquities of the West, she was interrupted by the appearance at the door of a large, bearded man in his forties dressed in a checked shirt and oversized jeans held up by braces.

"Fritz, you take those muddy boots off before you come any closer!" She barked the instructions loudly to her husband.

Fritz sighed but did as he was told. He embraced his cousin Hans and greeted Martin with a firm handshake. Over breakfast Hans explained again how Martin had decided to come back to Germany and was keen to find work.

"Well, Martin. We could always do with some help on the farm if you're up to it?" said Fritz. "What sort of work did you do before?"

David hesitated. He could hardly say he was once a corporal in the British Army and was used to driving Chieftain tanks but had now decided to defect.

"Oh, I did lots of different things."

Fritz said nothing but looked at him expectantly and David realised he would have to give him more information based on his new identity.

"In the States I turned my hand to anything – taxi driver, construction worker, waiter. You know what it's like in America – people let you do anything provided you're willing to work for peanuts."

Neither Fritz nor Helga had any idea what it was like in America. They had never had any inclination to travel abroad even if that had been permitted by the authorities and the farthest they had ever been from Wilschdorf was a weekend they had spent in Leipzig just after they got married.

Seeing Fritz's evident disappointment in his answer David knew he had to appear more enthusiastic and so he added, "but believe me, I want to work. I can drive a tractor and help around the farm in any way you want. The one thing I am good at is shooting – hunting rifles, handguns, you name it. I won prizes for it, I did."

Fritz brightened at this.

"Ah, a fellow hunter. I'm glad to hear it. You must join our local Schützenverein. We meet every weekend and now is the hunting season. We have lots of animals in the surrounding forests. You should join us too, Hans."

"Not really my thing, Fritz," said Hans as he got up from the table. "And now, my dears, I'm afraid I must go. I have an appointment in Dresden at midday, but I shall be back soon." He then smiled at David and clapped him on the back. "Fritz and Helga will take good care of you, my friend."

After breakfast David was shown to his room which contained a comfortable single bed, a wardrobe, and a desk. It was basic rustic accommodation, but it was still better than the barracks he was used to. Fritz then took him on a tour of the farm which grew sugar beet and rye and boasted a herd of fifty cows which provided them with milk and cheese most of which they sold on to the cooperative. By East German standards they were well off.

Over the next few weeks David gradually got used to the farming life. He drove the tractor and learned how to herd and milk the cows. He joined the Schützenverein where he impressed the locals with his shooting prowess. He went hunting with Fritz in the forest where they shot deer and wild boar which they sold on to the local butcher. The daily work on the farm was hard and Fritz and Helga welcomed the extra pair of hands. They had never had children and so they appreciated having a young man around the house. His presence brought out the maternal instinct in Helga who fussed around her ginger haired boy as though he were her own son.

Fritz was a member of the party and was well regarded in the village as a solid communist. Two months after his arrival David was taken to a meeting of the local committee in Dresden where he was introduced to various members of the party hierarchy. By this time his stumbling German had improved in fluency, and he was able to explain how he wanted to work for what he termed "the cause" of socialism. His audience, dour apparatchiks to a man, were, however, less impressed by his political commitment than by his reputation in the Schützenverein as a marksman. In East Germany politicians were ten a penny while a good shooter was a real asset.

By the time the New Year came round, David began to feel at home in his new environment. He enjoyed farm work and the company of Fritz and Helga whom he began to regard as friends. He took pleasure in the regular hunting expeditions and relished the frequent praise he received from his shooting companions as to his ability as a huntsman. Although he missed some of his friends in the army and regretted not having any contact with his mum Evie, it was a blessing to be able to live without the incessant orders of superior officers. In short, he was beginning to realise that he was now more Martin Hauptmann than David Mould.

Hans did not return to visit them at the farm until the beginning of February when he drove up late one morning in his Trabant followed by a second car – a black Soviet-made Zhiguli – out of which stepped a Russian officer. Hans greeted Helga and Fritz and introduced the officer as Lieutenant Colonel

Platov who had heard everything about Martin and was interested in meeting him. As they all sat down around the kitchen table the major smiled but said nothing as Fritz obsequiously offered them beer.

"Ah, Radeberger pilsener! My favourite local beer," said the Russian as he sipped appreciatively from the beer mug placed in front of him.

Fritz smiled. It was not every day that you had a visit from a Russian officer. After a few pleasantries about the weather and the journey from Dresden, Hans asked if he and the Russian colonel could be left alone with Martin. Nonplussed and not a little worried, Fritz and Helga withdrew. Martin was confused and was beginning to think that he might be arrested. He had never met a Russian before, but he had heard stories about the way prisoners might be treated in the East and he was, after all, an illegal alien.

"There is nothing to worry about, Herr Hauptmann." The officer spoke quietly and smiled again at Martin who thought that the man seemed even shorter once he had taken off the peaked cap of his uniform. What he lacked in physical stature, however, he made up for in the calculating stare of the ice-cold blue eyes.

"I can assure you that we have no desire to take you into custody nor to accuse you of anything." His German was good with only the faintest trace of a Russian accent.

"On the contrary, Hans has told me of how you came to be in the German Democratic Republic and of how you wish to be of service."

There was a silence while the Russian looked intently at Martin and Hans nodded in agreement. This was obviously an important person, thought Martin, who deserved the usual respect due to any military officer.

"Well, yes, sir. I do want to be of use. I believe in what you socialists are trying to do here. Make society better for the workers. And if I can help in any way......"

Hans smiled at that. He had mentored his recruit well.

"I am sure you can, Martin," said the Russian slowly, "but you must understand that at any moment we could take you over the border and give you back to the British authorities. I think you'd be in a lot of trouble, no? So, in some way, you see, you owe us."

"I realise that, sir."

Martin was beginning to sweat. Being handed back to the British Army was the last thing he wanted. He was not afraid of being ill-treated but the process of being labelled a traitor, cashiered from the army, and probably imprisoned for some years, was not something he wished to contemplate.

"Well, let us see what you can tell us and in what ways you can help."

They spoke for almost two hours while Fritz and Helga hovered outside the kitchen door hoping to hear snatches of the conversation and worrying that they too might be arrested. Martin told the officer all about his life as David growing up in south London, how he had lost his father (he omitted to mention he had murdered him) and then joined the army at his mother's insistence. He spoke about his friendship with Hans and about that dark, rainy evening when his friend had been crushed by a tank on exercise and he had finally realised he wanted a new life. He said how pleased he was to be living in East Germany and how much he enjoyed his shooting expeditions at which he thought he had shown a particular talent.

At the end of the interview – for that is what it was – the Russian officer stood up and thanked Martin for his time.

"It has been a pleasure meeting you, Herr Hauptmann. I suggest that you keep what we have discussed between you and me. No need to bother your friends with it. I shall be in touch through Herr Fiedler."

He put his cap back on, shook Martin's hand and turned to go while Hans went to find Fritz and Helga to say goodbye. At the door he stopped and turned to face Martin.

"Have you ever seen the Russian television series The Shield and the Sword?"

"No, sir."

"You should watch it if you can. It is very good. It is what inspired me to join the service. It is about a Russian spy who infiltrates the German Abwehr in the Second World War. It shows how the actions of one man can change the fate of millions. You too could be such a man. Goodbye, Herr Hauptmann."

They watched the two cars drive off with quite different emotions. For Fritz and Helga, it was with palpable relief that they had not been taken away by the Stasi to an indeterminate fate in some Dresden prison. Martin, on the other hand, was left bemused and intrigued by the visit. What help did the Russian officer envisage he could provide? Who was he anyway? What service did he work for? He asked Fritz.

"You don't know?" He looked astonished at Martin's ignorance and then added in an awed whisper, "He's KGB, of course."

Martin had been briefed on the activities of the KGB as part of the British army training for deployment to West Germany, but this was the first time he had come face-to-face with a member of the Russian secret service. It was with a mixture of surprise, trepidation, and pride that he realised with a start that he was being recruited. For what reasons he was yet to find out.

Later that day, back in the KGB offices on Angelikastrasse in Dresden, the Russian officer sat at his desk and mulled over with Hans the outcome of the conversation.

"An interesting contact you have made, Hans. I shall commend you to Moscow Centre."

Hans beamed with pleasure at the recognition of his efforts. He knew that one of the main duties of the KGB offices in Dresden was to recruit potential assets, particularly foreigners, who could be used in the future in the interest of the Soviet empire.

"You will maintain contact with him, of course, and he may be required to undertake some training which I shall arrange. He is young but I think he can be manipulated. Overall, a useful asset. Congratulations, Hans."

Once Hans had gone, Lieutenant Colonel Platov spent the rest of the afternoon composing a confidential report to Moscow

Centre recommending the designation of a certain Martin Hauptmann, formerly corporal David Mould of the British Army, as an asset of the KGB in East Germany to be used, after the requisite training, in fulfilling any task, legal or otherwise, which might be required by the Kremlin. He added that the asset's apparent expertise with guns might be a useful attribute in any covert operation, particularly abroad.

It was getting dark by the time he had finished the report. He was pleased with his work and was sure that Moscow too would approve. He had added another pawn in the complicated chessboard of relationships with the West. He had as yet no idea how it might be used but that would come later. But by now his wife, Lyudmila, and his daughters would be waiting for him. He signed the report with his real name – Vladimir Vladimirovich Putin.

CHAPTER 8 – Berkshire and London 2001

"Get back to your fucking whore in London! And you can rearrange those words in any way you want, you bastard." With that she hurled a plate at him from one side of the kitchen to the other. It missed his head by inches and exploded against the wall scattering fragments of porcelain over the Aga and across the tiled floor. It was an expensive Royal Copenhagen dinner plate, part of the dining service they had received from her parents upon their wedding only two years before.

"Calm down, Helena!"

He knew it was the wrong thing to say as soon as he said it. He also regretted leaving the bills out for the flat. She had not known about it nor about how much it was costing. She had come across them that Saturday morning and nuclear fission had resulted.

"Calm down? You utter shit. You ask me to calm down when you've gambled away most of our money, we're on the brink of bankruptcy and you still carry on with that trollop. You've even rented a flat for the bloody bitch. Fuck you!"

This time she threw a particularly fine Wedgewood milk jug which hit him full on the chest before shattering on the floor. She was now in a rage she could hardly control, her red hair spiking in anger so that she looked like some deranged harpy. It was time for him to leave. Breakfast was clearly out of the question. He barely had time to get through the kitchen door before he heard her yelling after him as yet another piece of tableware broke.

"I shall go and see the solicitor first thing Monday morning. This is going to cost you dear, you bastard."

As he took the Jaguar down the driveway from their substantial Edwardian home in Ascot, he had to admit that she was right. He had behaved abominably but then he had always considered himself genetically predisposed to infidelity just like his father and grandfather before him. Then again, he reflected, she knew what he was like when she married him. It was her second marriage after her first husband had died unexpectedly of a heart attack. It was his third and he supposed that he was now facing yet another expensive divorce.

John Peregrine Amherst had inherited his father's construction firm at the age of thirty. Despite an expensive education at Winchester, he had failed to get into university and began working for his father when he was just eighteen. He was not, however, by nature a businessman and upon his father's death left most of the running of the company to the chief executive while he devoted his efforts to spending the dividends he received and pursuing his political aspirations. He had been elected as a Conservative MP in a safe seat at the age of forty and hoped for a ministerial post if the party won the next general election. He had now been waiting five years for the elevation to shadow minister but if he could not get his finances in order, hopes in that direction would recede fast. His company already owed the banks substantial sums which he could not cover, he had debts from gambling on the horses and now he risked losing the house in Ascot which he had mistakenly put in his wife's name as part of the marriage arrangements. It was not then surprising that he felt thoroughly depressed as he arrived in the pouring rain at his Mayfair flat that morning in early April.

Molly, his mistress whom he had installed in the exorbitantly expensive rented flat near Grosvenor Square, was a glamorous blond fifteen years his junior and an aspiring actress with little talent. She was at a rehearsal for some obscure German play in a North London theatre, so he had the place to himself. He exchanged his suit, which smelled of the musty community centre where he had held his boring constituency meeting the day before, for jeans, a casual shirt and jacket and sat down in the living room with a large brandy and a cigar. He smoothed back his thinning hair carefully and first phoned his lawyer.

"Charles? I'm awfully sorry to bother you on a Saturday morning. I'm afraid I'm going to need your services."

There was an imperceptible sigh at the other end of the line. It was not the first time that Charles Ingram had been asked to act for John Peregrine Amherst and he had known for a long time that the current extramarital affair of his client was bound to end in tears one day.

"I take it Helena is asking for a divorce?"

"Not in so many words but she's seeing her lawyer on Monday morning."

"Well, John, we know the ropes, don't we? Are you going to contest it?"

"I can hardly do that, can I?"

"I suppose not. I presume the main issue will be money."

"That's the thing, Charles. I don't actually have much at the moment. The company has a temporary cash flow problem, and the banks won't lend me anymore. I was wondering if you knew of anyone who might be persuaded to extend me a short-term loan."

"How much are we talking about?"

"Two or three million."

"Jesus Christ."

There was a long silence while Charles pondered how he could advise his client. The fact was he did not like John Amherst very much. He had known him since his first divorce and considered him feckless, irresponsible and, if he were asked to give an honest opinion, not very bright. He had been amazed when he was elected as an MP, but he supposed that the party considered him a safe pair of hands who could be relied upon to spout unthinkingly the political mantras of the day. On the other hand, it was not for him to make judgements and he always owed a client the best advice he could give.

"Leave it with me, John. I'll put out a few feelers and get back to you early next week."

It was the best that John could hope for. He then phoned the party leader's office on the pretext that he wanted to discuss the position on an immigration bill which was due to be debated in the House on Monday. He wanted to show how interested and knowledgeable he was so that he might be considered at the right time for the shadow Home Secretary position. The office informed him rather curtly, he thought, that the leader was on a trip to a marginal seat in the north of England and would not be back until late Sunday evening.

He was disappointed at the attitude of the leader's office. Did those hacks not realise what an asset he would be on the frontbench? He poured himself another brandy and briefly considered phoning the company executive, but he had had enough bad news for one day and watched television instead until Molly came back from rehearsal.

After the debate in the House on Monday during which he was dejected at again not being called on to speak, he returned to the flat thoroughly disgruntled and even more worried about his future. At eight o'clock Charles phoned.

"John, I may have good news for you. A friend of mine has been in contact with someone who might be persuaded to provide you with a loan. On commercial terms, of course, you understand."

"Of course, that goes without saying. And may I ask who this person is?"

"He's a Russian currently living in exile in London. Apparently, he's got some problems with the authorities in Moscow and has made a request for asylum in the UK. I gather he's quite rich and, in addition to agreeing a personal loan, he might even consider a donation to the party. It would be a feather in your cap if he did. Anyway, he is willing to meet you. Shall we say the Carlton at seven o'clock this Thursday evening?"

The Carlton club is an exclusive member only establishment in St James's founded in 1832 by the first Duke of Wellington for what is now the Conservative party. Ivan met his lawyer, Matthew Davidson, at the entrance at six thirty in the evening and they were directed by the reception to wait in the foyer while a call went out to John Amherst.

Ivan doubted whether the meeting would be useful, but he was now in need of any help he could get in expediting his asylum request which had now been languishing with the Home Office for a year. His own MP had been less than enthusiastic in pleading his case having railed against the government in the House at the number of Russian oligarchs who had taken up residence in what was now commonly termed Londongrad. If a loan to this John

Amherst could oil the rusty cogs of British bureaucracy, then so be it. He had researched Amherst's construction company which had a turnover of about a hundred million pounds a year and debts of seventy at a time when the building industry in general was in the doldrums. He knew that any loan was likely to be risky.

"Not very good prospects," Matthew had commented laconically.

"Depends how much he wants," replied Ivan as he watched with interest the exits and entrances of the club members. He recognised a few MPs and peers, some of whom seemed old enough to have been there since the club's founding.

Just after seven John Amherst appeared with his own lawyer, Charles, and they repaired to the bar where they sat in leather armchairs and nursed glasses of brandy. John, who was already on his third glass, launched his pitch with a smile.

"It's good of you to see us, Mr Galishin."

"It's Goloshin," said Ivan drily.

"Yes, yes, of course, sorry. My Russian's not particularly good these days." John chuckled while the others remained silent, and Charles sighed inwardly at his client's patronising tone.

"Well, the thing is, my company has a very promising portfolio of building projects but planning permissions are slow. Building regulations are so bloody difficult these days, you know. Not helped by the current government. What I'm looking for is a short-term loan, say six months, just to tide us over a very temporary cash flow situation. I must emphasise, very temporary."

"Won't the banks help?"

"Ah, these bank managers! You know what they're like. No vision. No imagination. All they see is numbers while I see a glorious future for a prosperous company. All I need is an investor who shares that conviction."

John was by now waving his brandy glass expansively as though wafting away the army of petty bureaucrats who were stifling him as the embodiment of British industry.

"And how much would this loan be?"

John had thought about this for some days. He had no intention of paying off all his company's creditors, but he did need enough to settle his gambling debts and the result of the divorce proceedings during which Helena was bound to want to ring him dry.

"As I see it, twenty million should see us through this."

Charles raised his eyebrows. That sort of figure far exceeded what he had discussed with his client.

"On a purely commercial basis, of course," added John reassuringly. "If you agree, Charles and Matthew here can sort out the paperwork and we can sign the agreement tomorrow. There is a slight, how shall I put it, urgency. I can also put in a good word for you at the Home Office. I have some sway there, you know, and I understand you are still awaiting approval of an asylum application."

It was a lie, of course. The idea that an obscure opposition backbencher with no standing in his own party could have any influence on a decision by the Home Secretary in such a case was preposterous and they all knew it.

Ivan sipped his brandy and looked at John intently. He was reminded of the numerous negotiations he had had with the corrupt politicians in St Petersburg. He now had the measure of a man who was clearly desperate for a cash injection. His lawyer was right that it was unlikely that the loan would be paid back on time or in full. On the other hand, it might be useful to have someone on his side in Parliament.

"That's a lot of money, Mr Ambridge."

"Amherst, actually," said John, slightly taken aback.

"Yes, of course, sorry. My English not so good." Ivan smiled knowingly.

"I tell you what I'll do, Mr Amherst," Ivan put his half-finished brandy down and leaned forward. "Here is my business card with my home address and telephone number. Let me consider your proposal with my lawyer. I'll get back to you as soon as I can. You can contact me anytime but give me a few days, yes?"

The four of them stood up and shook hands. John was visibly deflated as he watched Ivan and his lawyer exit the club along with the prospects for his financial rescue.

"I don't think that went well, John," said Charles.

"Fuck!" That's all that John could think of saying as he made his way back to the bar. He had not, however, given up hope. He would ring the Russian in a few days' time.

John consoled himself with one more brandy before taking a taxi back to the flat. Molly was at another rehearsal and Helena was away for a few days at her mother's, no doubt plotting her revenge. John intended to take advantage of her absence from the marital home in Ascot to pick up some of his things.

He drove the Jaguar and arrived at the house just after nine. It took him less than an hour to pack a suitcase and retrieve the cheque book and a few documents from the office. He knew he had had too much to drink but reckoned he could get back to Mayfair safely and avoid the police by taking the smaller country roads into London.

He turned the volume up on the car radio to keep himself awake and kept the speed down. A fine drizzle was falling, and the tree-lined roads around Ascot were unlit so he found it difficult to clearly see the road ahead. Suddenly a dark shape appeared in front of the car, hit the bumper with a loud thump, and bounced off the roof. He jammed on the brakes and slewed the car to the right where it slid to a halt on the grass verge. It must be a deer, one of those bloody muntjacs, he thought as he switched off the engine and got out of the car unsteadily to see where the animal had fallen. Looking back up the road he could see it lying at the foot of the tree. He approached cautiously, unsure as to whether it was still alive.

"Oh, my God!"

The body he saw was not a deer, but a young girl dressed in a raincoat and a red bobble hat. He realised with horror that she was dead. Her head lolled at an impossible angle, and she was clearly not breathing. She had evidently ricocheted off the car against the tree and died instantly.

He looked up and down the road unsure of what to do. There was no one about and no traffic. No sound but the rain falling and the wind whispering in the trees. What the hell was a young girl doing wandering about country roads at this time of night? He knew he should report it but that would be the end of his career. In fact, the end of everything. He would not be able to avoid a conviction and a lengthy prison term at the end of which he would have no job, no money, and no prospects for anything - not even redemption. He knew there was only one decision he could take. He walked back to the car and drove back to London.

The body was discovered the next day by a passing motorist. The report was announced in the local news on Saturday morning:

'A local girl, Gillian Smith, aged fourteen, was found dead on Friday morning at 1045 am on Mill Lane near Sunninghill, victim of an apparent hit-and-run. The family is distraught at the loss. Police have no leads yet but are still

pursuing enquiries and have asked for any
witnesses to come forward.'

CHAPTER 9 – April 2002

He could just make out the cliffs of Dover from the upper deck of the Channel ferry as it began the crossing from Calais at eleven o'clock in the morning that second week in April. It was a fresh spring day. The sun was shining, the sea was calm and above the hubbub of the passengers and crew he listened to the gulls crying in the vessel's wake.

David was not by nature sentimental, but he could not avoid a slight pang of nostalgia for the old country. It was almost fifteen years since he had set foot in England and he realised with some surprise that, for better or worse, he was now a foreigner with a German passport in the name of Eberhard Wagner, born April 1967 in Stuttgart. It was just one of several aliases he used on the job. Deep down inside just below Martin Hauptmann he knew there still existed a certain David Mould, but that person had become just the smallest doll in the nest of a Russian Matryoshka. He set aside these fanciful thoughts as he went down to the bar and ordered a lemonade. The crossing would take an hour and a half, so he had time to relax.

After the interview in 1988 Lieutenant Colonel Platov had kept his word and had arranged a series of training courses for David with the Stasi in Dresden designed to nurture his shooting skills and introduce him to the several ways that a "special operative" could be used to eliminate enemies of the state. During this time David continued to work on Fritz's farm. He watched the television series recommended by the Russian officer and dreamed that he too could become a spy. He would fight for the socialist cause and help to bring down the capitalist system of the West. He would receive medals from the Russian authorities and be fêted by generals. He felt he finally had a purpose in life.

He was aware, of course, that he was also being groomed by the KGB to be an assassin and that, if he were ever used in that capacity, he had the advantage for the Soviet authorities of plausible deniability. They could never be held accountable if the perpetrator turned out to be a British national who had defected to East

Germany. On the contrary, they could just as easily contend that he belonged to MI5 or MI6. He knew that if he was ever caught, he would be left high and dry. David was not, however, bothered with these thoughts and enjoyed his special status with the KGB office in Dresden and the admiration of Fritz and Helga who saw their lodger as a committed communist and a friend of the Kremlin.

The fall of the Berlin Wall in November 1989, however, changed everything. David's training ceased and he lost contact with the KGB agents whose office on the Angelikastrasse was vacated by March 1990. Even Hans seemed to have disappeared and no longer visited his cousin's farm in Wilschdorf. By the beginning of 1991 David had assumed that he would never be called upon by his Soviet friends. East Germany had been absorbed within a reunified Federal Republic of Germany and, much to the disgust of Fritz and Helga, would now enjoy the benefits of the capitalist system. The Cold War was over, Eastern Europe was at peace and David reconciled himself to his future as a farmer.

It was late morning on February 12, 1992, that Hans made a surprise visit to the farm and asked to speak to David. They embraced each other like long-lost brothers.

"Martin, mein Freund, it's been a long time."

"It has indeed. We were beginning to think you'd disappeared forever."

Hans sighed and shrugged his shoulders as they sat down at the kitchen table to drink a beer together.

"It has been a challenging time, Martin. Too many changes and not all for the best."

"And what of our KGB friends?"

"Oh, they all returned to Russia but not happily, I dare say. The Communist Party is now banned, the Soviet Union no longer exists, and Boris Yeltsin is president of a new Russian Federation. God help us."

Hans fell silent and turned disconsolately to his beer. He then pulled himself together and smiled at David.

"But we must not dwell on the bad things. How's life treating you?"

"I cannot complain. I enjoy the farming life and I have been champion shooter of the Schützenverein for two years running."

"Good to hear that." Hans paused as though debating how to broach a subject.

"In fact, it's very good to hear that. You see, I still keep in touch with our former KGB friends, and they have a favour to ask for which you will be paid handsomely."

As David sat in the bar on the Channel ferry ten years later, he recalled that first assignment. He was asked to "remove" a member of the Tambov mafia who was guilty of numerous crimes in St Petersburg including embezzlement, extortion, and murder but who had managed to escape the Russian justice system thanks to incompetence and corruption. He had made millions through a chain of brothels in St Petersburg and the import of cocaine. That was what Hans told him, anyway, and David had no objections in principle to murdering someone who was so obviously a criminal and an enemy of the state.

It had been a straightforward mission. The target was Igor Ivanov who was on holiday in the seaside resort of Benalmedena near Malaga in Spain. Hans gave him all the details of the hotel where Ivanov was staying and provided him with plane tickets, a false passport and two thousand euros. He arrived one summer day in Malaga late in the morning and took a taxi to the hotel where he booked in for five days. His room had a small veranda overlooking the beach where thousands of tourists were sunning themselves. He spent three days observing the target's movements sometimes with the aid of binoculars.

Igor Ivanov was a creature of habit. He spent his evenings in the bars or casinos and his days on the beach. Every morning at ten he would waddle down in his swim trunks to the sands in front of the hotel carrying a towel and settle himself in a deck chair just in front of a bar. He was a large, overweight man with a glutinous beer gut that testified to a life of excess. At about eleven o'clock he would order the first drink of many from the bar and then return to the beach. Through his binoculars David could see that it was always a cocktail or perhaps a gin and tonic.

The question was how he was going to carry out the deed. Shooting from his hotel balcony was out of the question. For obvious reasons he had not been able to bring his sniper rifle with him on the plane and, even with a silencer on the handgun he had picked up in Malaga, the death was in any event likely to cause pandemonium amongst the sunbathers and an immediate police lockdown of the area. He might not be able to escape from the hotel in time.

He could push him off the balcony of his hotel room. They were both on the tenth floor and his KGB trainers had told him that such a method was often used. However, he would first have to gain access to the room and then wrestle with 150 kilos of a Russian bear before heaving the body over the rail. David had always kept fit, did not smoke or drink but even for him this was a tall order. It was out of the question. That left poison as the only option.

Most of these required a close relationship with the target and took too long to work even if he had access to them which he did not. But he did have a phial of potassium cyanide crystals which he had been able to bring unnoticed through customs.

On the fourth morning at the hotel, he followed Ivanov down to the beach in his swim trunks and sat a few metres away from him ostensibly determined to get a suntan. The blue Mediterranean dazzled in the warm sunshine. Just after eleven Ivanov went to the beach bar and came back with what looked like a Long Island iced tea complete with a pretty coloured paper umbrella in the glass. David waited half an hour and then went to the bar and ordered the same. By this time Ivanov had almost finished his drink.

"Señor, por favor. De la gerencia."

David proffered the glass with the compliments of the management. Ivanov looked confused at first and then smiled and nodded his thanks as he took the second iced tea. David's Spanish at that time was not good, but it was sufficient to persuade the Russian that he was just a waiter from the bar. No one had seen him dissolve the cyanide crystals into the drink.

David walked back to the hotel. He had already packed his suitcase and paid his hotel bill. Before leaving he took a moment to look through his binoculars from the balcony. On the beach he could now see a huddle of concerned tourists around Ivanov who had tumbled off his deckchair and was now writhing in agony on the sand. He had given him six hundred milligrams and Ivanov would be dead in five minutes. He took a perverse pleasure in watching him die. It was the same feeling he had had when he killed his father.

David had undertaken a total of fifteen assignments over the ten years since that first assassination for each of which he had been rewarded with a handsome payment. In addition to Ivanov, three more had been in Spain which became a favourite basking place for Russians who had got rich under Yeltsin's free market economy in the 1990s. One had 'accidentally' fallen from a hotel bedroom in Estepona; one was shot while skiing in the

Sierra Nevada and another had an unfortunate car accident when his brakes failed on a mountain road behind Malaga. The other hits had been carried out in France, Italy, and Germany.

He had employed a variety of methods – guns, knives, explosives, poison, or simple physical power – but always with a view as to what was appropriate to the circumstances and what would allow him to escape the crime scene undetected. A bomb on the Paris Metro which had taken the life of a prominent Russian dissident had been blamed on an obscure Corsican terrorist group. A member of the Russian Mafia was shot dead in the back streets of Naples in what was attributed to a revenge killing by the Camorra. Another had drowned in the river Isar in Munich despite being an expert swimmer. David prided himself on meticulous forward planning and faultless execution. He was aware that, however terrible it might seem, the act of killing provided him with a sense of accomplishment just as it had on that day when he stabbed his father to death.

His professionalism was obviously appreciated by his handlers since he now had a substantial nest egg of over one million euros in a savings account at a local Dresdner bank. He had also been lucky since he had never been caught.

He never questioned who exactly ordered the contracts – he assumed it was the Russian secret services although it could equally be rival criminal gangs. The targets were always communicated through Hans on his visits to the farm, but he never divulged the instigator nor the precise reasons why the person in question had to be eliminated. Similarly, Fritz and Helga never enquired of David as to why he would sometimes disappear "on business", content to assume that he was undertaking important tasks for the cause.

At the beginning he felt no guilt for these killings. For the most part they appeared to be gangsters like Ivanov who already had blood on their hands and deserved to die. He liked to think he was simply a surgeon clinically excising bad tumours from society, operations in which he tried his best to avoid any collateral damage to innocent bystanders. Gradually, however, he had surprised himself by recognising the growth in him of a conscience. The last three targets had subsequently appeared to be simple Russian businessmen who had made the mistake of being overly critical of their own government. Killing criminals was justified in his mind since it was simply taking over where the legal system had failed. Killing those who simply disagreed with the system might not be.

By the time the ferry docked in Dover, David decided that this would be his last contract. He recognised that by now he might be addicted to his trade, but he was tired and wanted a long rest. Perhaps it was time for him to settle down, to marry and start a family. That was clearly out of the question if he continued his career as an assassin. He had had girlfriends in Germany but no relationship serious enough for him to contemplate marriage and the example of his parents had always put him off the institution. It would also have been problematic to explain to a wife his mysterious business trips. Yes, he concluded, once he had finished this mission he would retire.

He took the train to London and then travelled by taxi from King's Cross to Cricklewood Broadway. Although it was now fifteen years since his defection, he worried that the authorities might still be after him and he wanted to avoid being picked up by a surveillance camera on the tube system. For the same reason he had grown a moustache and dyed his hair black. He booked into the Crown hotel and told the receptionist that he might be staying for a week or two. Hans had given him the address of the target in Hampstead, but he did not want to stay in the same area as the man he was about to kill. He needed to take time to monitor his target's movements and to decide how he would do it. Before that, though, there was something else he had to do.

It took three buses to travel down to Millwall the next morning, but David sat contentedly on the top floor of the double-deckers through Hyde Park and Peckham and wondered at how much and yet how little

London had changed. There was more traffic certainly and more construction particularly around Canary Wharf and many of the streets in south London he knew as a boy had now been improved. But while money had flowed into some areas, the poor were still around and the council houses on the street where he once lived still looked tired and neglected.

He hesitated for a long time before he knocked on the door. Over the years he had sent birthday and Christmas cards to his mother with limited information but always from a different location in Germany for fear that they might be traced back to Wilschdorf and he had never told her exactly where he lived. Consequently, he did not even know whether she was still alive. He had disappeared as a young English soldier and was now returning as a middle-aged German. If she was alive, would she even recognise him?

It took a long time for the door to open and then it was only pulled ajar so that David had difficulty hearing the voice of his mother Evie.

"Who is it?"

"It's me, ma. It's Davey."

"Who?"

"Davey. Your son."

There was a long pause and then the door opened fully. Evie looked at her son in disbelief, her eyes wide, trying to take in this tall, dark stranger who stood before her. She stood back from the doorway and sat down quickly on a chair in the hall.

"Oh, my God. It can't be. What the bloody hell have you done to your hair?"

"It's me, ma, I promise you," said David, laughing to cover his tears of joy and moving forward to give her a hug. He would never have believed he could be so pleased to see his mother alive. At this Evie burst into tears and squeezed her son so tightly he could hardly breathe.

Son and mother spent three hours together and consumed innumerable cups of tea while they exchanged news. Alfie was still on the scene, he heard, but Evie said she would never marry again. David's sisters were all married by now and there were nine grandchildren who made her happy after all the years she had suffered with Sid. David explained his dyed hair by saying sotto voce that he was working undercover for the German government, and he got Evie to swear that she would keep his visit secret. He told her that he had made a life for himself in Germany and that it was unlikely he would ever be able to come back to England. He promised, however, that he would keep in touch.

"As long as you're happy, son. That's all that matters to me," said Evie, folding her hands over his and smiling at him through her tears.

He left his mother on the doorstep of the house he had grown up in and looked back just once to see her waving goodbye. She seemed so small and grey to him like a faded picture in an old photograph. He felt an emptiness in his heart and knew at once that he would never see her again.

He took the buses back to Cricklewood and ate a solitary meal in the hotel restaurant. From tomorrow he had to concentrate on the task ahead – how to kill the oligarch Ivan Vladimirovich Goloshin.

CHAPTER 10 – London

The phone rang at two in the morning of November 14, 2001. Ivan had only just got to sleep in his house in Hampstead and was due in court at ten. He stretched his arm out to the bedside table and fumbled for the receiver. There was a clatter of static before the Russian voice came through.

"Ivan Vladimirovich?"

"Speaking. Who is it?"

Half asleep, Ivan had a sudden feeling of panic. It could be the secret services. It was just the sort of thing they would do, waking up citizens in the middle of the night.

"It's Grigor. Grigor Petrov, a friend of Sergei Tikhonovitch. We met when you were in St Petersburg. I'm ringing from Moscow."

Grigor Petrov. Ivan tried to clear his head and then remembered vaguely the fresh-faced young lawyer whom Sergei had taken on as one of his interns. He looked at his watch. It was five o'clock Moscow time.

"I'm sorry to ring so early but I thought you should know as soon as possible."

"What is it?"

"Sergei is dead."

There was a long pause while Ivan tried to take in the news. Sergei, his oldest friend, the boy with freckles he played with when they were growing up in St Petersburg, his companion on the law course in Moscow and his business partner for many years. He had not spoken with him since his return to London but there was no suggestion that he had been ill.

"My God! How did he die?"

"The authorities in St Petersburg have issued a statement. It happened on Monday night. Apparently, he threw himself off the roof of the Astoria hotel. Doctors have attested to the fact that he was suffering from depression and was also being treated for narcolepsy. My sincere condolences, Ivan Vladimirovich."

Narcolepsy, depression. It was preposterous, thought Ivan. Sergei had never fallen asleep during meetings and, as far as he was aware, had never walked in his sleep. He was also probably the least depressed person he had ever known. Any setback in life or in business was usually met with a laugh and a glass of vodka. He was a bon viveur who enjoyed life too much. Then he realised that this was, of course, no suicide. Like him, Sergei had been a vocal critic of the regime, and this was the way you stifled opposition – by simple elimination.

Ivan could not sleep the rest of the night. Despite the time of night, he phoned St Petersburg and spoke to Sergei's wife who was distraught at the death of her husband. He then called mutual acquaintances in Moscow and London. They were all shocked, but they all came to the same conclusion. This was the work of the FSB.

He broke the news to Irina at breakfast. She cried at the loss of someone who had been almost an uncle to her and immediately telephoned Alexei, Sergei's son, who was still at Cambridge doing a PhD.

Ivan spent the morning in court in central London listening to yet another deposition from the Russian Federation in support of his extradition. Lack of sleep and the news of Sergei's death contributed in his case to a mounting depression and a feeling that he was sliding down into a vortex of impossible obstacles from which he would never escape. On top of tax evasion and fraud he was now being accused with embezzlement of state funds. Even the judge was having difficulty keeping up with the mountain of allegations against him. The only consolation was that the more charges were levied against him the more protracted the legal proceedings would be.

At the beginning of December, friends of Sergei Tikhonovitch who lived in London – for the most part Russian expatriates, exiles like Ivan, wealthy businessmen, and asylum seekers – arranged a gathering in commemoration of his life which took place one afternoon in the Promenade room of the Dorchester on Park Lane. For obvious reasons none of those there could have taken the risk of going back to Russia for the funeral service.

Ivan and Irina took Peter with them. The occasion was attended by fifty or sixty guests including the oligarchs Boris Berezovsky, who was seeking political asylum in the UK, Vladimir Gusinski who had flown in from exile in Spain, and Mikhail Khodorkovsky, the richest man in Russia and said to be worth over ten billion dollars. Peter also noted the presence of Alexander Litvinenko, the former FSB officer who had been granted asylum in the UK the year before and who had written numerous magazine articles accusing the Russian secret services and the Putin regime of a litany of nefarious practices including assassination.

It was more a wake than a memorial service just as Sergei would have wished it, with copious amounts of champagne and vodka flowing in celebration of his life. It was also, thought Ivan, a way to reassert humanity in face of the actions of the secret services. Peter had other thoughts as he looked around the room and realised that the combined wealth of the attendees was more than the GDP of many countries of the world.

The death, or rather murder, of Sergei had a greater effect on Ivan's disposition then he would admit to. He became morose and bad-tempered. He was happy that Irina had taken up her place at King's College to study law and that she had found a steady boyfriend in Peter, but these thoughts were only a partial compensation for the continuing pressure of his legal battles and his increasing fear that one day the FSB would come after him. On the morning of the first day of the New Year 2002, Ivan made finally a resolution to change his life.

It was two o'clock, the party had come to an end, kisses, and wishes had been exchanged and most of the guests had left. Irina had made all the arrangements and the celebrations had gone splendidly. Caviar and lobsters had been consumed in quantity along with many bottles of fine wine and champagne. At midnight a raucous rendition of auld lang syne had ended with fireworks in the garden that lit up Hampstead Heath. No doubt there would be complaints from the neighbours about noisy Russians, chuckled Peter as he sat next to Irina on the sofa in front of the Georgian fireplace. The only other people left were Ivan's lawyer, Matthew, and his financial advisor, a dapper young man in an Armani suit whose name was Bruce Haslehurst. Both sat in armchairs cradling tumblers of brandy. Ivan himself stood between them in front of the Christmas tree with a glass and a bottle of vodka looking like the best man at a wedding about to give a speech. It was the happiest Irina had seen him for weeks.

"мои дорогие, с новым годом! My dear friends and my beautiful daughter, I wish you all a happy New Year. And to my dear departed wife, a kiss from those who are still down here." With that he looked heavenwards, downed a shot glass of vodka, and smiled at them all beatifically.

"I know you should not make New Year's resolutions. They never last and even if they do, they usually end in tears. But I have made one and I intend to see it through."

They looked at him expectantly, wondering just how drunk he was and whether he would suddenly burst out singing some patriotic Russian song.

"I have done many wrong things in my life, and I now want to set things right. This year I intend to get poorer and to do something useful with my money."

He left the words hanging in the air while they all wondered what he meant and then went on.

"I want to set up a foundation for the education of poor children. I shall sell the estate in Hampshire and the flat in New York. Together with the money I have in shares and bank accounts here in the UK there should be enough to provide a capital fund of around 400 million pounds. I should like my daughter Irina to be the director. There'll be plenty left over for her inheritance when I die and enough for me to live on for as long as I've got. I should like Bruce and Matthew here to put the arrangements in place as soon as possible."

They all looked at each other in surprise.

"Ivan, are you sure you want to do this?" asked Bruce.

"I'm sure. It's what Natasha would have wanted."

"But why exactly? And why now?" added Matthew.

"Because I'm tired, Matthew. I'm tired of this endless struggle with the Russian Federation. Tired of business. Tired of the courts and the justice system. I'm tired of looking over my shoulder wondering whether I'll be the next victim of the FSB or if my daughter might be kidnapped. And you know what? It's all to do with money. Putin and his cronies are determined to bring down the oligarchs and reward their friends instead – the siloviki, the strongmen who will take over Russia."

"But surely Putin is better than Yeltsin. Bush and Blair seem to have every hope that Russia is moving to a peaceful and stable democracy."

Peter was aware of the articles both Litvinenko and Ivan had written against the Russian government but wondered whether these had not been exaggerated. He also realised that there was a profound sadness in Ivan. He was consumed with guilt that he was so rich while others were so poor.

"Ah, Peter. I wish I shared your optimism. But I don't and I can't. The politicians in the West are blinkered. Most Russians don't want a democracy. They are not used to it. They just want a strong man in charge and a quiet life. And Putin will be that man. But believe me, we are sleepwalking into a nightmare. Sergei knew that and look what happened to him."

There was a silence while everyone contemplated what Ivan had said. Then Irina got up and gave her father a kiss on the cheek.

"Papa, you must do what you think is right and what mama would have wanted."

By March 2002 things finally started looking up for Ivan Goloshin. The exasperated English judge had finally ruled that the Russian Federation's case for his extradition was unfounded and based largely on a tissue of flimsy allegations. He denied the right to appeal. He even hinted that the Kremlin's prosecution of the case bordered on a malicious vendetta. The Russian authorities huffed and puffed but there was little they could do. Although Ivan's request for asylum was still being bounced around by bureaucrats in the

Home Office, this judgement was a cause for celebration. The establishment of the Natasha Goloshina education foundation was also making progress and for the first time in years he felt optimistic about the future.

Ivan enjoyed living in Hampstead. It was far enough away from the hectic bustle of central London to have retained a rustic village gentility, a sense of peaceful Englishness which he relished after the political and financial chaos of St Petersburg. Two mornings a week he took to walking down to a café on Heath Street where they sold French pastries and a good espresso. It was rather pretentiously called Au Petit Beurre and tried to emulate a Parisian boulevard establishment by putting out chairs and tables whenever the sun shone. The café had pretty awnings in blue and white stripes extending over the pavement so that on a warm summer day it might have passed for an establishment in Le Touquet. They went so far as to produce the menu in French although the waitresses had difficulty pronouncing some of the words – brioche usually sounded like brooch. Nevertheless, it had a charm of its own and the proprietor, an attractive brunette in her forties from Uxbridge called Daphne, got used to seeing this tall, handsome Russian who always ordered double espressos, tartines and a pain au chocolat and tipped extravagantly.

He usually met friends at the café. Sometimes his lawyer, Matthew, but more often than not they were fellow Russians like him. One was Dmitry Fyodorovich Semyonov, a retired academic in his sixties who lived nearby and was writing a biography of his great-grandfather who had fought for the Whites against the Bolsheviks during the Russian Civil War in the early 1920s. Dmitry's father had left Russia as a young man during Stalin's purges in the thirties and set up a bookshop in London which his son had then inherited. Dmitry was a gentle soul, a slight man with silver hair and a goatee beard who had a mine of stories and anecdotes about Russia even though he had never actually lived there. But he had a Russian soul and that, as far as Ivan was concerned, counted for everything. He delighted in their conversations together.

It was the last Thursday in April and a fine spring day. Ivan had arranged to meet Dmitry for coffee at ten o'clock. He walked up the Vale of Health and took a turn on the heath before retracing his steps into the village. One of his bodyguards, Boris, followed him at a discreet distance. Ivan had not yet had the courage to dispense with his security. He might have won his legal case against the Russian Federation, but this did not mean the FSB was no longer a threat. In fact, he suspected that his win in the English courts had probably increased it.

He sat down at a table outside the café and waved to Daphne who came out to take his order. He briefly noticed the man in a hat, raincoat and gloves who had sat down at a nearby table just after him with a Waitrose bag by his feet. He wondered for a moment why the man should be dressed for winter when the sun was so warm but then, he supposed, Hampstead had many eccentrics, and a badly dressed tramp could often just as easily turn out to be a famous Shakespearean actor.

Dmitry arrived five minutes later. They began chatting about the latest news in Russia

- Putin was tightening his grip on power by removing all the communists from committees in the Duma. Ivan's mobile phone suddenly rang and, apologising to Dmitry, he walked twenty metres up the road to answer it. It was Matthew with a technical question about funding for the foundation. Turning round to look back at the café, Ivan was vaguely aware that the man in the hat had now departed leaving his Waitrose bag and made a mental note to himself to tell Daphne.

The explosion happened just as Ivan was finishing his conversation with Matthew. The sound was deafening, and the force of the blast threw him on the ground. The front of the café had been blown out with tables, chairs and shattered glass strewn to the other side of the road. The blue and white awning was in tatters on the ground spattered with red. He heard the screams of passers-by and cars crashing as he sat up to see the wreckage in front of him. A shard of glass had cut his forehead and he tasted blood. Boris was immediately at his side to make sure he was all right and helped him stand up. Apart from a few cuts and bruises he appeared to be unhurt. That was not the case with Dmitry whose body lay face down and motionless on a gradually reddening pavement scattered with French pastries. His clothes had been shredded and his left arm had been ripped from his shoulder from which blood was still pulsing. It was his blood on the awning. Even before he could check, it was obvious to Ivan that Dmitry was dead.

Miraculously none of the staff at the café had been seriously hurt although they were all in a state of shock. Daphne had had the presence of mind to call 999 immediately. The local police arrived with blaring sirens within ten minutes and an ambulance shortly after. Three paramedics tried their best with Dmitry, but it was in vain, and he was declared dead at the scene. The area was cordoned off with tape as an army bomb disposal team arrived followed by another three police squad cars half an hour later out of one of which stepped a middle-aged man with a beard and a young woman. They walked over to where Ivan was now sitting on a chair holding his head.

"Are you all right, sir?" asked the woman.

"He was my friend. Why would they do this?"

"What is your name, sir?"

"Goloshin. Vladimir Goloshin."

"Can you tell me what happened? What do you mean by 'they'?"

It was the senior officer. Ivan recognised a Scottish brogue in the voice and struggled to put his thoughts together.

"It was so sudden. I was finishing a phone call when it happened. We were having a cup of coffee together. He was just a poor old man in the wrong place at the wrong time."

"And who do you think might be responsible, sir?"

Even in shock Ivan did not need to reflect for a moment. It was obviously the man in the raincoat and hat.

"It was the FSB. The bomb was in the bag. The Waitrose bag."

CHAPTER 11 – April 2002

Superintendent Trevelyan Hamish McIntosh, known as Hamish to his friends, had been with the Metropolitan police counterterrorism unit for ten years. He had been in army intelligence in Northern Ireland during the troubles of the 1970s before joining the police and then moving from Scotland to London. His English mother, who hailed originally from Somerset, had insisted on giving him the first name Trevelyan over the objections of his Scottish father and, more particularly, his paternal grandmother who detested anything from south of the border. Despite this he was proud of his Highland roots and retained his lilting Scottish accent in defiance of his London colleagues. Not that he resembled in any way the stereotypical grumpy Scot you might see on television programmes or on film. On the contrary, he was of a genial disposition with a ready sense of humour. Perhaps this had been cultivated as an antidote to the sorts of criminal terrorists he had met in his job - he found they were invariably unhappy people who had converted the chunky chips on their shoulders into outright hatred and who were willing to sacrifice mindlessly any number of innocent lives in support of a cause.

He got to work at around eight o'clock that Thursday morning expecting a quiet day. He ran a team of ten detectives who had been monitoring the activities of several suspected terrorist cells - Al-Qaeda and IRA mainly - but intelligence had dried up and there was no expectation of any imminent attacks. Perhaps he would have a quiet weekend with his wife in Barnet mowing the lawn and pruning the roses. At six foot six he strode through the offices and beamed at his colleagues through his naval beard.

"Good morning, ladies and gentlemen, and what a beautiful spring morning it is."

They smiled back at him. He was lucky to have such a bright and diligent group – eight men and two women – all of whom were dedicated to the job. He said good morning to his secretary, Pamela, and settled down at his desk to sift through his correspondence. He had no meetings that day and was looking forward to not having any senior officers breathing down his neck.

At precisely 1105 there was an urgent knock on his door and detective constable Anoushka Khan rushed in.

"Sorry, Chief. We just had a call. There's been an explosion. About half an hour ago. In Hampstead. Looks like a bomb went off. One fatality reported. Local police and emergency services are there, and bomb disposal is on its way."

"Hampstead!" Hamish was incredulous. There had never been any indication of any criminal gangs or terrorist cells in Hampstead. Had they missed some intelligence?

"Nothing ever happens in Hampstead."

"Well, Chief, looks like something happened this morning. Do you want to leave it with the local police, or should we attend?"

"No, we'd better see what's going down. Call a squad car and get your skates on – you're coming with me."

Even with the sirens on it took half an hour to get up to Hampstead. Hamish was glad to have Anoushka with him. She was the brightest star in his team. He admired her feisty independence. Originally from Pakistan, her father was a doctor and her mother a pharmacist and they had both expected her to take up medicine. Perhaps out of rebellion she decided to do something different. She had taken a degree in politics from Manchester University and had chosen to join the police force to, as she put it, "make a difference." She certainly had the brains, thought Hamish, and he hoped without any real expectation that she would keep her optimism about any difference she might make.

As they arrived at the scene on Heath Street in Hampstead, they took in the mess the bomb had made. The local police seemed to have everything in hand and had taped off the area from one side of the road to the other. The bomb disposal unit was already sweeping for other devices and forensics was on its way. Police helicopters could be heard flying over the scene and there was a rumble of conversation from the local and national press which was beginning to gather outside the tape.

They spoke briefly to the man sitting on a chair outside the café. He was obviously in shock but seemed otherwise unhurt. He declined to be taken to A&E and, after speaking with the paramedics and ascertaining his address, Hamish decided he and his bodyguard should be taken home with the family liaison officer. They would interview them later. They went into the café and spoke to Daphne who seemed at first remarkably unaffected by the events. She told them how lucky she felt that she and the café staff had all been at the back of the shop when the bomb went off and had escaped the full effects of the blast.

"It happened about twenty past ten. It was a quiet morning. Not many customers and not many other people about, thank God. We just had the two gentlemen who come here every week. I think they're Russian. Real gentlemen they are and good tippers too. I'm so sorry about the poor man who died."

She was suddenly overcome by emotion and began to cry.

"Why would anyone do such a terrible thing?" she sobbed.

"And there was no one else in the café?" asked Hamish.

"No." Then suddenly she had a thought.

"Oh but wait a minute. Yes, now I remember. There was another man sitting at a table outside. I hadn't got around to serving him when the bomb went off. He was wearing a hat and a raincoat."

"Was there anything else you noticed about him?"

"Not really. He wasn't there for long, and you couldn't see the face because of the hat."

"Well, thank you, Miss er….?"

"Hamilton. Daphne Hamilton."

"Well, thank you Miss Hamilton. You'll be asked to come down to the police station, of course, to give a full statement. In the meantime, I'm sorry about all this. We'll do our best to find whoever did this."

He was about to exit the café when another thought occurred to him.

"Do you, by any chance, have any surveillance cameras?"

"No. Can't afford that sort of thing."

Hamish came out of the café and looked across the street over the heads of numerous police officers who were combing the area for clues together with forensic officers in white overalls who were now picking up pieces of glass and fragments of the bomb. A BBC cameraman was now filming the scene and a reporter was recording for the news bulletins. He looked at Anoushka thoughtfully.

"I can't believe this is Al Qaeda's work, still less the Real IRA. Doesn't make sense to set off a bomb in Hampstead of all places." Then he noticed a small surveillance camera on the wall of Barclays bank across the street.

"I need what they've got on that camera, Anoushka. We need to get whatever we can from forensics and bomb disposal when they've finished. I need to know the makeup of this device, whatever it was. Tell them it's urgent.

Ask the team to review the info on all possible terrorist cells in London and whether there have been any claims of responsibility for this attack. This could be the first of several. Tell them to contact MI5 to see if they have any leads. Let's set up a crisis meeting in the office at four. Oh, and ask them to get me an appointment with the commissioner after that. This'll hit the evening news and he'll need to be briefed. But first we're going to have a wee chat with this Russian and his bodyguard. They seem to be the only eyewitnesses we've got."

He turned back to the squad car with a sigh of resignation realising that his quiet weekend in the garden had now been deleted from the calendar.

The interview with the bodyguard and the Russian at his home did not provide much in the way of tangible clues. The man himself had obviously been shaken by the event and was adamant it was an assassination attempt by the Russian secret services as revenge for his criticism of the government. Hamish was not convinced. Such hits were normally more subtle. He recalled the poisoning in 1978 of the

Bulgarian Georgi Markov with a ricin pellet injected from an umbrella. That was more their style. But he told himself to keep an open mind.

They spoke to the daughter, Irina, who had left her lectures at university as soon as she had heard of the bombing and a young man who was obviously her boyfriend. He took his name and address and noted to himself that he would have to investigate his background although he discounted the likelihood that he might be involved in the bombing.

At the crisis meeting back at the Met later that afternoon he reviewed with his team the little information they had got so far. No known group had claimed responsibility although it was early days. In general, however, intelligence indicated that terrorist groups had been quiet in the UK since the last car bombing by the Real IRA in Ealing in August 2001 and no one could reliably attribute the bombing to anyone.

"The bomb disposal guys have told me that the device was probably RDX or hexogen. They're still confirming," announced Anoushka.

"Apparently, it was used in the assassination of Rajiv Gandhi in 1991."

"Well, we'll have to find out where you can buy this stuff. It's obviously not on sale at Tesco's," Hamish smiled grimly.

"By the way, chief, I got the videotape from Barclays bank. It's down at the photo lab. I'll review it later today. You'll also want to tell the commissioner that the name of the man who died was Dmitry Semyonov. He was 68 years old and a historian. We're not releasing the name to the public until the next of kin are informed."

When the commissioner was briefed at 5 o'clock that afternoon, he appeared almost irritated that London's peace had been disturbed as though it was Hamish's fault that a bomb had exploded in Hampstead and a man had been killed.

"I'll have to inform the Home Secretary," he said regretfully. He hated bringing unwelcome news to politicians which might reflect badly on their policies to reduce crime, as though they could wave a wand and change the nature of Homo Sapiens at a stroke. Unfortunately, they invariably blamed the messenger.

"Yes, sir," said Hamish refraining diplomatically from any further commentary.

The bombing made the headlines on the BBC News at six o'clock with pictures of the destruction of the café in Hampstead and comments from journalists speculating that this could be the start of another wave of terrorist attacks. The Met could not provide anyone to be interviewed – the commissioner had a dinner that evening – and restricted itself to a bland statement that no one had yet claimed responsibility, that there had been one fatality and that investigations were ongoing.

****

David Mould watched the news on the television that evening in his hotel room in Cricklewood and swore several times. Having left the bomb outside the café, he had walked down Heath Street binning the hat, raincoat, and gloves on his way. He had turned to watch the explosion from two hundred yards distance and then, like others, had approached the scene pretending to offer help but really to make sure he had hit his mark. He saw one body lying on the ground in front of the café and then a man stumbling towards it whom he recognised at once as the target. The bomb had missed him. He walked down the road away from the chaos along with many other people fleeing the scene and took a taxi back to his hotel.

He had spent two weeks monitoring the movements of Ivan Goloshin; watching the back of the house from the Heath with binoculars while pretending to be birdwatching; following him and his bodyguard at a discreet distance as they walked down to the village for a morning coffee. He always wore different clothes and a change of hats and always travelled over from the hotel by taxi or bus. At the end of this time, he had concluded that the only sure way of killing the oligarch was a bomb. Not a letter bomb – he could not be sure of the recipient. Poison was ruled out – he would never get near enough to the target – and shooting with a sniper rifle from the Heath, although possible, was fraught with difficulties, not least of which was having to conceal himself while waiting for the target in an area frequented by numerous dog walkers.

He had used bombs before. They were quick and effective and only small amounts of RDX were needed for an individual target. Collateral damage was, of course, possible but he could live with that. He had procured it from a sleeper cell in Shoreditch, the address of which Hans had given him. He had added a sniper rifle and a stiletto knife to the order to maximise his options. He had packed the explosive and the timer in a small white box tied with a red ribbon and placed it in the Waitrose bag. If anyone had seen it, they would have assumed it was an Easter egg. The timer switch was located on the bottom of the box and set for ten minutes. He had had to transport the deadly package three times on the bus from Cricklewood to Hampstead before conditions were ideal. He had to make sure that the target was there at his usual café and that there were few people about. At last, he had his chance that Thursday morning.

Wearing a hat and raincoat he had followed Goloshin and his bodyguard and waited until the target had sat down at the table outside the café. He had worn gloves to avoid any chance of fingerprints being left. He then took his place at a nearby table and switched the timer on. He left one minute later and walked down the road. Everything should have worked out fine. But he had not anticipated the arrival of the elderly man, nor that the target would leave the table just minutes before the explosion. All the planning had gone to waste and Goloshin was still alive.

He used a public phone box to call Hans that evening after the news to tell him that the attempted assassination had failed. Hans had already seen the pictures on German television and heard press speculation that this was the IRA. He knew, however, that this was Martin's contract and that he had failed.

"I'm sorry but I could not deliver the parcel."

"That's a great pity, Martin. My friends and I had every faith in you, and they will be extremely disappointed. If you need anything you can contact our friend in Shoreditch. You will try again?"

There was a moment's silence David considered his options and realised he had none. Those he served demanded results and there was no knowing what they might do if he did not deliver. This was his last contract and he now had to see it through to the end.

CHAPTER 12 – April 2002

The call came through to Peter's office just after midday on the day of the bombing. Irina sounded distraught.

"Oh, my God, Peter. They've just tried to kill my father."

"Jesus Christ! What's happened?"

"It was a bomb. Papa was having coffee with an old friend of his in Hampstead. His favourite café. There was an explosion and his friend, Dmitry Fyodorovich……" Irina stifled a sob midsentence, "He's dead, Peter. They blew a poor old man to pieces."

"What about your father?"

"He's not physically hurt. Just a few cuts and bruises but there's no doubt he's in shock. We thought we'd be safe in London." Irina began to cry quietly not only for the man who had died but also for the dream of a peaceful life which had now been shattered.

"Give me half an hour and I'll be up there."

Peter took a taxi from the office and arrived at the house forty minutes later. Two police constables standing outside the gate checked his identity before ringing the bell. Both bodyguards, Boris, and Yuri, were patrolling the grounds and the maid opening the door to the house looked ashen faced. Irina appeared a moment later and Peter gave her a long hug of comfort before they went into the library to see her father.

"Ivan Vladimirovich, I'm so sorry about what has happened."

"Ah, Peter, it is not for you to feel sorry. I suppose it was bound to happen someday. They know where I am, those bastards in the Kremlin. They never forget and they never forgive."

Ivan sat despondently in an armchair by the fire. To Peter he seemed shrunken by the experience.

"Are you sure it was the FSB?"

"What does it matter?" replied Ivan irritably. "The Cheka, NKVD, GRU, KGB, FSB. Russia has had secret services since before

Catherine the Great. You can go back as far as the oprichniki of Ivan the Terrible. Every so often they change the name but what they do has always remained the same. They are there to protect the tsar or the state from the individual and they will do anything necessary to achieve that aim. I know I was a target and I have been stupid to think that I could be safe here."

Irina came to kneel at her father's feet and took his hand.

"It's not your fault, papa."

"What will you do?" asked Peter.

"We cannot stay here in England. That much is clear. There is no doubt they will try again. We have another set of passports we can use. Perhaps if we move to Spain? What do you think, Irina?"

There was a long silence while Irina considered the prospect of moving again, of leaving her law course, of leaving England and the man she had fallen in love with. Was she destined to spend the rest of her life on the run? To be always in fear for her life and that of her father? She looked at Peter and smiled sadly. Since the death of her mother, she had always been there for her father for both consolation and moral support. She knew that there was no way she could let him face an uncertain future on his own.

"Peter can always come with us," added Ivan. He now realised clearly that his daughter was seriously involved with this Englishman and that it would be unfair to ask her to give him up. At the same time, he knew that she was as much a target as he was and that he needed to do everything possible to protect her. Peter looked at Irina and knew he would have a decision to make.

The conversation was interrupted by the doorbell and the housekeeper entered announcing the arrival of superintendent McIntosh and constable Khan who proceeded to go over the events of the morning with both Ivan and Boris. They also took Peter's name and address. He decided not to tell them where he worked. At least not at this stage. The fact that he was employed by MI5 might have added another unnecessary red herring into the mix. Peter already realised that the police were not wholly convinced that the bomb was an assassination attempt by the FSB.

"Thank you for your time, Mr Goloshin and I'm sorry for your loss," said Hamish as Ivan walked him back to the front door. "We may need to come back later as we pursue our enquiries. We shall leave the police constables outside the gate for a few days. Just in case, you know."

"I have my own bodyguards, Inspector, so there's no need."

Did they really think two policemen constituted a deterrence, thought Ivan. Against the FSB which had all the means of the Russian Federation at its disposal.

"I take it that I am not under arrest or anything. And that I can travel if necessary? I'm a businessman and need to attend meetings."

"Of course not, sir. You are a victim in this case, and we intend to get to the bottom of it. I would, however, ask you to inform us of your location in case we need to get in touch."

Ivan watched as the two police officers pushed through the gaggle of press outside the gate and drove off in the squad car. The paparazzi were jostling to snap a picture of the oligarch who had almost been killed. The press had recently lost interest in Ivan's articles and interviews critical of Russia – the West was now bending over backwards to accommodate the new regime, to give Putin the benefit of any doubt and in any event the public had had enough of such stories. But a bomb attack in Hampstead from which a man had barely escaped with his life, and which had blown his friend's body to pieces, now that would sell newspapers.

By the time he had returned to the library Ivan had made up his mind. He would fly out to the villa in Spain as soon as it could be arranged. He told Irina and Peter and left it to them to decide whether they wanted to come too.

A moment later the phone rang. It was Matthew, his lawyer.

"My God, Ivan. I've just heard the news. Are you okay?"

"Yes, thank you. A bit shaken, that's all."

"If there's anything I can do, you just have to say."

"Thank you, Matthew. I appreciate it. I've decided to fly out to the villa in Spain. At least for a few days. Give me time to think, you know. I may need your help in tying up a few things here."

"Of course, just let me know what you want me to do."

There was a pregnant pause while each wondered what the other was thinking. Until now Matthew had never completely bought into Ivan's conviction that he was under threat of assassination which he sometimes thought bordered on paranoia. He was a rich man, of course, but compared to other Russian oligarchs had surely never amounted to more than an irritating thorn in the thick hide of the Kremlin. The bombing in Hampstead was now giving him second thoughts and, as his client, he would do everything to help him. For the moment, however, he decided to change the subject.

"You'll be pleased to know that we've made substantial progress in setting up Natasha's foundation which should be up and running in a month or two. I just need your and Irina's signatures on several documents to legally establish the trust."

"I'm glad to hear that," said Ivan distractedly.

"There's one other thing I should mention."

"Yes?"

"I'm being pestered by Charles Fullerton. You remember the lawyer for Mr John Amherst, the MP? We met them both at the Carlton club in December. He's still interested in negotiating a loan for his company and would appreciate a meeting if you have time. After what you've been through, I'd quite understand, however, if you chose to have nothing to do with it."

Ivan thought for a moment. He had no desire to meet the impecunious MP again but, as his asylum request had still not been granted, it might still be worth having an ally in the British establishment.

"No, it's all right. I'm willing to meet him. Tell him to come to the house in Hampstead. Just him, not his lawyer. The last thing I want is some legal mumbo-jumbo. Sometime Monday morning. If he can't make that he can come to Spain if he has a serious proposition. My office can arrange it. I can at least hear what he has to say."

Ivan returned to the library to say goodbye to Peter who had to return to work. His muscles ached and his bruises hurt. He felt tired and dispirited. He realised that, despite all his wealth, he could not continue to live like this. He had to get away and extract himself somehow from this spider's web of fear. He poured himself a vodka and began to plan his flight to Spain.

Irina saw Peter to the door and kissed him goodbye.

"You understand, don't you, that I must go with him. I can't abandon him now."

"I understand."

"You can come with us. You know I love you, Lensky."

"I love you too, Olga."

He smiled at the use of their affectionate sobriquets, but his mind was in a turmoil as he took the tube back into central London. He felt he was being sucked into a surreal film plot over which he had no control. A fantastic game of treachery and assassinations in which he was just a pawn. Was he really going to flee England? What did Ivan mean by another set of passports for him and Irina? Were they going to travel under false identities? If so, was he aiding and abetting breaking the law? Would he also become a target? Would he be arrested?

These conflicting thoughts jumbled around in his brain that evening as he shared a bottle of wine with his flatmate Jeremy who was characteristically blunt.

"It seems quite straightforward to me, Peter. If you love the girl, go. If you have doubts, stay. Carpe diem! But don't, for God's sake, dither!"

In the event, the decision was effectively taken by others. On Friday morning he was unexpectedly summoned to the office of the director-general. This was not something that often happened to lowly members of the service and Peter had never met the head of MI5.

"Peter, do sit down." The director-general did not get up but indicated a seat. Silver haired and bespectacled, he looked more like a college history professor than the head of Britain's security services.

"Your head of Department, James Greenwood, tells me you are close friends with Ivan Vladimirovich Goloshin?"

"I'm not sure I would use the phrase 'close friends,' but I do know him and his daughter well."

The director-general fixed him with piercing grey eyes and thought for a moment.

"Let me say at the outset that I'm sorry about the events of yesterday morning. It was a terrible attack and the police and the security services are doing all we can to find out who was responsible. If you see Mr Goloshin, I should be grateful if you would pass on my sympathy and deepest condolences on the loss of his friend."

"I will do, sir."

"You are aware, of course, that Mr Goloshin is a person of special interest to us largely because of his outspoken opinions about Russia."

"I am aware of that."

"You will also know that relations with Russia are particularly sensitive at the moment for both us and the Americans. The continuing problems in Chechnya, the unrest in the Middle East not to mention the considerable Russian investments and money in the UK economy. All these factors need to be borne in mind when we assess our relationships with the Kremlin. And I have to say that there is nothing to indicate as yet that the events in Hampstead have anything to do with the Russian secret services and we would not want them to be blamed unfairly, would we?"

He looked again intently at Peter as he paused and weighed his words.

"It would be unfortunate if Mr Goloshin were to say things to the press which were not founded on facts. We don't want to muddy the waters, do we? Too many cooks and all that. You understand what I mean?"

Peter nodded and wondered how many more platitudes the director could come up with. Of course, he understood. UK and USA Inc wanted Ivan to keep quiet, not to upset the various diplomatic, military, and economic apples in the barrel, preferably not to speak to the press at all.

"Well, Peter, perhaps you'd like to have a word with Mr Goloshin and invite him to take a low profile – in his and our interests."

So that was it. MI5 wanted to use him to silence Ivan. He was to be a pawn in their chess game. By the time he had got back to his office he had decided he did not want to play. Since he suspected that he too might be under surveillance he used a public call box on the way home to phone Irina to tell her he would be coming to Spain with them. He went back to the flat and composed a resignation letter to MI5. It was the end of his career but this time it was he and not God who had thrown the dice.

CHAPTER 13 – Sunday 27 April 2002

There were times when detective constable Daniel Cooper regretted joining the police force. Being dragged in for a case review by the superintendant on a wet Sunday morning after too many beers the night before in the Kings Arms in Peckham was just such a time. He was just dozing off at his desk when he was shocked awake by the familiar strident Scottish voice.

"Wakey wakey, Daniel! I know none of you want to be here but we've a killer out there and it's our job to apprehend him as soon as possible before he commits another attack."

Hamish had assembled all his team to establish what stage they had reached in their investigations. Daniel was the first to go.

"Well, sir, we conducted twenty-three interviews – the shop owners on either side of Heath Street near the café. They all confirmed what the owner of the café, Miss Hamilton, has already reported. That just before the explosion there were three people sitting outside the café

– Mr Goloshin, the victim Mr Semyonov and a man in a raincoat and hat who has yet to be identified. No one saw this man clearly, but he appears to have been of medium build, about six foot tall with black hair and a moustache. Not a lot to go on."

"What about forensics?" asked Hamish.

It was constable Elliott Fraser's turn.

"They confirm that residues found at the crime scene indicate it was RDX or hexogen. They reckon about a pound of the stuff was used and probably detonated with a timer. Everything seems to point to it being left by this man in a raincoat and hat. They got a lot of fingerprints from the café itself but nothing to go on for the moment."

"Any leads on organisations that might be responsible?"

"We contacted MI5, MI6 and GCHQ," said constable Stevenson, "but nothing so far. No one has claimed responsibility and there's been no recent activity by the usual suspects – Al Qaeda, IRA, or the Real IRA. There's been a lot of press speculation, of course, that it could be the Russians especially since that's the nationality of Mr Goloshin but that has been denied categorically by the Kremlin's press office."

"Well, laddie, they would do that, wouldn't they?" said Hamish dismissively. "They'd deny their own grandmother's existence given half the chance. What about the video camera?"

"We got hold of two videotapes," said constable Khan. "One from Barclays bank across the road and another from a jeweller further down. They both cover the whole period and area of the explosion. They're not too clear but I'd like you to see them, sir, if you have time."

"Right ho, Anoushka. Let's have a look then."

Hamish dismissed the rest of the team and went to the back office with Anoushka where there was a video recorder and a television. She played the tapes one after the other at full and then at half speed. The one from Barclays bank clearly showed the arrival of Ivan Goloshin, Dmitry Semyonov, and the man in the raincoat outside the café. The latter placed a Waitrose bag by his table and left shortly afterwards. The camera was located some fifty yards from the café, but Anoushka had had a still blown up from the video which showed a man with black hair and a moustache.

The video from the jeweller had less detail about the café and the explosion itself but covered a period five minutes after that during which a tall man could be seen walking up the road towards the crime scene. He no longer had the coat or hat, but the black hair and moustache clearly indicated that it was the same man. More importantly, Anoushka had produced a grainy still from that video too which showed the man's full face.

"Good work, PC Khan. At least we might have a picture of a suspect."

"I sent the photo off for comparison with all the databases we know but there's been no match with any information held by the police forces, MI5, MI6 or GCHQ."

"Not surprising, really. It would have been a long shot."

"Then I had a thought, sir. My brother's in the British Army and I know they have photo records too, so I sent it to them on the off chance and am waiting for a call back."

Hamish went back to his office. He had several cases underway, but the Hampstead explosion was by far the highest profile, and he had to complete a report on it to the commissioner by Monday morning. Half an hour later constable Khan knocked on his door.

"I just had MOD on the phone. You're not going to believe this, chief."

"Trust me, Anoushka, nothing would surprise me."

"Well, MOD reckons this could be a man they've been after for years. Apparently, a corporal David Mould went AWOL in West Germany during a British Army exercise in 1987 and was never seen again. The RMP still have him on their books as a deserter. He was ginger haired then but apart from the black hair and the moustache they think this could be him. In disguise."

"Sounds a bit far-fetched to me. What's he been doing for the last fifteen years?"

"I've got a theory, sir."

"Okay, let's hear it."

"Well, what if this corporal had been abducted by the East Germans? This was before the Berlin wall came down if you remember. They had kidnappings and spies all the time. My theory is that this man was trained in East Germany, probably by the KGB, to be an assassin, a hitman for the Russians and he's been working for them under cover all this time. This would fit in with Mr Goloshin's conviction that the FSB was out to get him."

Hamish could not help admiring his constable's evident enthusiasm for such a preposterous story which might have made a good plot for a spy novel or a TV series but was hardly likely to impress the commissioner. He was about to dismiss it out of hand when he remembered Sherlock Holmes's guiding principle for the work of a detective – when you have eliminated the impossible, whatever remains, however improbable, must be the truth. Anoushka's theory sounded improbable, but it might just be true.

"I suppose it's possible," said Hamish sceptically. "Let's pay another visit to Mr Goloshin. We can take the photos with us and see what he thinks of your theory. Give him a ring and ask him if we can see him at his house tomorrow morning."

Hamish would not have been sceptical had he known that at that very moment the improbable hitman of Anoushka's theory was walking on Hampstead Heath less than ten kilometres away from the Met's offices in New Scotland Yard. He was wearing a flat cap and a plastic raincoat to ward off the April showers. From time to time, he trained his binoculars on the back of Goloshin's house which was barely a hundred yards away. He had a clear view of the French windows of the library as well as the courtyard on the right-hand side and the driveway to the road beyond. Having failed with the bomb, he had to try with the sniper rifle. He wanted to find the best vantage point from which to take a shot. He would not attempt this on a Sunday – there were too many people out jogging or walking their dogs – but would come back the next day. From behind the bushes at the edge of the heath he had raised the binoculars to take one last look when he heard a loud querulous voice behind him.

"Just what do you think you're doing?"

David turned to see an elderly lady dressed in a brown beanie hat from which long grey hair cascaded over a navy-blue duffel coat. She was holding an umbrella and a leash at the end of which was an ugly looking schnauzer who had obviously been to the same hairdressers as its mistress and who was growling menacingly. David pushed his way back from the bushes through the undergrowth to address the woman.

"Oh, I'm a birder. I've just seen an osprey, would you believe?"

"I hardly think that's likely. They're not native to Hampstead." The woman peered at him suspiciously through thick round spectacles as the dog began yapping aggressively. She might be short-sighted, but she could recognise a sexual pervert when she saw one.

"I think you're a peeping Tom. You'd better get going or I shall call the police."

David had no time for an argument, so he walked away with an expletive hurled over his shoulder. He would return the next morning and get it done. He was tiring of this contract which was proving much more difficult to carry out than he had first anticipated. He wanted to see Goloshin one more time just before he put a bullet through him.

That Sunday morning there was another man who wanted to see Goloshin but for quite different reasons. It had now been four months since John Amherst had broached the idea of a loan from the Russian oligarch with no progress despite numerous attempts on his part to get another meeting with Goloshin. His company, Amherst Construction Ltd, was now haemorrhaging money daily and was, in the typically concise phrase of his chief executive, Alfred Thompson, about to go "tits up".

"John, I'm telling you. We can pay the wages and our contractors for one more month and then that's it. We'll have to sack the workforce and file for insolvency."

"Alf, I'm trying my best. I've had meetings with five banks but none of them want to know. In the current climate they don't believe the value of our assets. God Almighty, I've even grovelled to that snivelling lump of protoplasm, the business minister, to see if we can get a government loan. He just sneered and said it wasn't the right time. Fucking Eton toffs."

As a product of another English public school, his alma mater Winchester, John Amherst was supremely oblivious of the irony of what he had just said.

"All I'm saying, John, is that if you don't get a cash injection pretty soon, we're done for."

John put the phone down and lit a cigarette. It was ten o'clock and he was lying in bed in the Mayfair flat next to the naked Molly who was snoring gently, blissfully unaware that her lover's whole life was unravelling. His company finances were not his only problem. Helena had submitted the divorce papers demanding ten million pounds and the house in Ascot. He knew she was bound to win. The only question was whether there would be any money left once the company went bankrupt.

The tabloids had got hold of the story of the divorce and were giving regular updates on the progress of the case under the general banner of "Opposition Sleaze," hinting at his multiple affairs. Somehow reporters had also got wind of his financial difficulties. All this bad press had not endeared him to the whips' office which had rung him up Saturday morning.

"I appreciate your interest, John, but there's no question of a position on the frontbench at the moment."

It was Jack Townsend, the chief whip and a northern MP who detested the southern yuppies like John who had recently, in his mind, adulterated the values of his party.

"Sort out this bloody divorce and get your finances in order and then we can speak again. Till then, John, I'm afraid your name is quite frankly toxic to the party."

Fucking toxic! So it's come to this, thought John, as he put the phone down barely able to contain his anger. He seemed to be assailed on all fronts since even his constituency committee, weary of the bad publicity their MP was getting, had begun to mutter about a recall motion to kick him out of his seat.

On top of everything he still had a nagging worry that the police might find out something that pointed to his responsibility for the hit-and-run on that Berkshire road in December. Fortunately, there had been no damage to his Jaguar. He was sorry for the poor girl who had died, of course, but he rationalised that sending him down for death by drunken and dangerous driving would do nothing to bring her back.

He slid out of bed careful not to wake Molly. He got dressed and went into the kitchen to prepare coffee. There was nothing for it, he thought. He would have to try Goloshin again. This time he would ask for thirty million. The man could afford it, surely. He knew he was worth almost a billion. He picked up the phone and dialled the number for Goloshin's lawyer, Matthew.

"Mr Davidson? It's John Amherst here. I'm so sorry to bother you on a Sunday. The life of an MP is so busy with Parliamentary and constituency affairs, you know, that it's difficult to find time for anything else."

He chuckled ruefully and hoped that his air of nonchalance would disguise the desperation he felt.

"Mr Amherst, yes, what can I do for you?"

"Well, you know the subject we discussed when we met at the Carlton club in December?"

"Yes, I remember."

"I was wondering whether you could facilitate another meeting with Mr Goloshin concerning a potential loan to my company."

"I'm not sure," replied Matthew guardedly. He knew of Ivan's intention to fly to Spain shortly and thought he might not want anything to do with the MP.

"I'd very much appreciate it if you could ask him."

John was aware that he had been too flippant and supercilious the last time and was determined now to be as sycophantic as necessary. He just needed the money.

"I'll see what I can do."

John's hopes were not high as the conversation ended but he realised that Goloshin's money represented a last resort. He had no other options left if this failed. He was, therefore, pleasantly surprised to have a call back from the lawyer a quarter of an hour later.

"Mr Amherst. Mr Goloshin is prepared to have a meeting, but it will have to be tomorrow morning at his house in Hampstead since he intends to fly to Spain in the afternoon. If that is not possible, I'm afraid you will have to come to Spain to see him. I'm sure Mr Goloshin might be prepared to put you up for a weekend."

Matthew thought that the prospect of having to fly to Spain to discuss a loan which might not even be agreed would put him off the idea.

John thought quickly. He was due to attend a parliamentary committee for his party that Monday morning which he could not afford to miss if he wanted to keep in with the whips' office. In any event, he liked the idea of spending a day or two at a millionaire's villa in Spain and enjoying the sun and a few bottles of wine. It would give him some respite from the mess of his life in England.

"I'm afraid I cannot make tomorrow morning, but I should be delighted to accept Mr Goloshin's invitation to come next weekend. Please convey my thanks to him."

John took down the address in Spain then went into the living room and poured himself a large glass of brandy. He had regained his optimism and was now buoyed up by the prospect of successfully negotiating the loan. He toyed briefly with the idea of taking the voluptuous Molly with him. After all, they both needed a break. But no, he decided, she would only get in the way. A delightful girl, good in bed but rather dim, he thought. In any event, there would be enough señoritas in Malaga if necessary.

CHAPTER 14 – Monday 28 April 2002

Hamish and PC Khan arrived at Goloshin's house at ten o'clock that morning. It was a bright spring day with the sun beaming happily over Hampstead. As they entered the hall, Boris the security guard was taking packed suitcases out to one of the cars in the driveway. Yuri had already departed to prepare the private jet for the flight to Malaga that afternoon.

"Good morning, superintendant. How can I help you?"

Ivan was less than pleased to see the police again. The sooner he could get out of England, he felt, the better. He had sent the maid home and told the housekeeper that they would be away for a time. He was sitting at his desk in the library putting his final signature on the documents Matthew had couriered over relating to Natasha's foundation and was now anxious to depart. Peter and Irina were standing by the French windows.

"I see you're planning a trip, Mr Goloshin?" said Hamish as Anoushka Khan took her pocketbook to write notes.

"As I explained before, I am a businessman and have to travel. I'm flying to Spain this afternoon with my daughter and Mr Johnson here. We plan to be away for a few days at least, perhaps a bit longer but I shall give you my address and phone number if you need to contact us."

"Thank you. Before you go, I should like you look at this photo. We believe it to be the man who was sitting in front of the café just before the explosion and who may have planted the bomb."

Hamish produced a photo of the man taken from the jewellers' video camera just after the explosion. Ivan studied it carefully.

"I wonder if you have any thoughts about it, sir. Do you recognise the man?"

Ivan looked at the photo again. The picture was indistinct, but he could make out a tall, medium built man with short black hair, a pencil thin moustache and a pallid complexion. He was dressed in a black jumper and jeans. He could have been anyone. He passed the photo to Peter and Irina.

"I'm sorry, inspector, I have no idea who this could be."

"That's all right, Mr Goloshin, it was a long shot anyway. You see…" Hamish hesitated and stroked his beard thoughtfully. He was still not convinced that the bombing was the work of the Russian secret services. It could just as well be the Mafia or any other criminal gang. After all, Goloshin was very rich and had probably made several shady deals and enemies in St Petersburg in the past. He decided, however, to put these doubts to one side.

"The Ministry of Defence has identified a man remarkably similar to this one who has been wanted for many years. He was a British soldier who disappeared while on exercises in 1987. PC Khan here has an idea."

Anoushka related her theory about David Mould.

"It's perfectly possible, I suppose," said Ivan. "The KGB actively recruited anyone they could during the 1980s. Mainly for spying but there's no reason why they could not have groomed someone to be an assassin. Especially a British national operating outside Russia. Would be a useful asset. The Russian secret services have never been anything other than inventive."

"There's something odd about this photo," intervened Peter handing it back to Hamish. "The hair looks unnatural, almost like a wig. Doesn't seem to go with the pale colouring of his face."

"You're right, Mr Johnson. In fact, the British soldier was ginger haired so it might be dyed."

Hamish was still not convinced and suspected that they might be barking up the wrong tree. The story seemed so far-fetched. Anoushka, on the other hand, was more than pleased that the Russian oligarch supported her theory.

"Well, Mr Goloshin, thank you for your time. I wish you a pleasant trip to Spain and we'll keep in touch if there are any developments. We are determined to catch this man, whoever he is."

Ivan, Peter, and Irina watched with relief as the police drove away. None of them thought it likely that the police would apprehend the bomber. He might already be back in Germany or Russia, thought Ivan. Or he might just be waiting for another opportunity. The threat was still there, and it was time to move.

The threat was, in fact, only a hundred yards away in the shape of David Mould. He had left his hotel in Cricklewood early that morning and had hidden himself in the bushes on the north-western corner of the heath at about nine o'clock. He had taken with him his Heckler and Koch sniper rifle which had a telescopic sight and could be carried in a small suitcase. He was satisfied that he could not be seen from either the house or the heath. There was no one about. Mothers were taking their children to school and fathers had already gone to work. He checked the sight on the rifle. He had a clear view of the back of the house, the courtyard, and the drive to the front gate. It was now just a question of waiting for the right moment.

He watched as two cars were moved from the garage at the rear of the property into the courtyard of the house. The first, a blue BMW, was driven off at about half past nine by a young man in a dark suit whom he did not recognise. Moments later a thickset man exited the house and seemed to check the second car, a black range Rover. He recognised the bodyguard. A middle-aged woman came out and handed him a package and went back in. He presumed it was a maid or housekeeper. But where the hell was Goloshin? He was beginning to lose patience. He was also worried that the longer he stayed the greater the chances were that he would be discovered.

He saw a police car arrive at ten and a man and woman enter the house. They came out half an hour later and drove off. The bodyguard then began loading the range Rover with suitcases and then sat in the driving seat. He suddenly realised that Goloshin was about to leave the house. He settled the rifle on his shoulder and prepared to fire. A young man and woman came out and got into the car. Suddenly there was Goloshin. It was now or never.

"What are you doing?"

David dropped the rifle in surprise. He recognised the voice. It was the beanie woman again with her dog. She had pushed her away through the undergrowth and now stood a few feet away from him.

"I said, what are you doing? You're the peeping Tom I saw the other day." she said accusingly as the schnauzer began growling.

"I told you I'm a birder, you stupid bitch."

"No, you're not," she said firmly as though admonishing a child at school.

Out of the corner of his eye he saw that the range Rover had now driven out of the gate. Goloshin had escaped him again. David could barely control his anger as he looked at the woman with her dog. For a split second he wondered whether to kill her and the dog there and then. But it would have made too much noise and left traces for the police to follow, he told himself. The most important thing now was to find out as soon as possible where Goloshin had gone.

"You're right, missus," he hissed to the woman. "I'm a serial killer and if you don't fuck off, you'll be next on my list."

He pushed his way past her kicking the dog who yelped and then began yapping. She stood back in shock and watched him walk away through the trees.

He walked off the heath and down the Vale of Health to Goloshin's house. He stood for a moment debating what to do and then rang the bell on the gate. There was an intercom that sparked to life.

"Yes, who is it?" It was a woman's voice. He assumed it was the housekeeper.

"Sorry to bother you, madam. It's the Metropolitan police here. Could I have a quick word?"

"Just a moment."

There was a buzz as the gate opened. He walked to the front door where the middle-aged woman he had seen earlier was now waiting.

"Your superintendant and his assistant have only just left."

"Yes, I'm sorry, madam, but they forgot to take the address where Mr Goloshin is going."

He flashed his passport in front of her so quickly that she had no time to read it properly. However, she had no reason to doubt his credentials. There had been so much police activity recently that she was getting used to their visits.

"Come in, officer, and I'll get it for you. If you'd like to wait here."

She beckoned him into the hall and disappeared into one of the rooms. She returned a moment later with a piece of paper.

"That's the address in Spain and the phone number."

"Thank you very much, madam." He looked in her eyes and paused for a moment.

"I'm sorry to bother you, but would you mind if I used your ablutions?"

"No, of course not. It's on the right."

In the toilet he took out the stiletto knife from the inside of his raincoat pocket. She would be able to give the police his description and he knew he could not let her live. He flushed the toilet and came into the hall holding the knife behind his back. She turned to open the front door. He grabbed her from behind putting his hand over her mouth and plunged the knife twice into her front under the ribs, making sure it cut into the heart and severed the aorta just as he had done when he killed his father so many years ago. She collapsed onto the floor with a gentle sigh. He waited a few minutes and then checked her pulse to make sure she was dead. As he closed the front door he turned briefly and looked at her. She looked so much like his mother when she was younger.

"I'm sorry," he whispered softly.

****

It was late that afternoon when the beanie-hatted Miss Hamilton-Smythe turned up at her nearest police station in Kentish Town to make a report about a dangerous sexual pervert she had met while walking her dog on Hampstead Heath. She asked to see the desk officer, Sergeant Braithwaite who she had often spoken to concerning the type of men she encountered on her morning constitutionals on Hampstead Heath.

"I'm sure he was a peeping Tom," she said. "It was the second time I saw him hiding in the bushes. I would have come earlier but Benji was not feeling well after the nasty man kicked him."

She bent down to pick up her weary schnauzer who seemed to sneer at the desk sergeant writing notes. She kissed the dog affectionately on his wet nose which made the sergeant wince in disgust.

"Would you like to give us a description, Miss, of the man?" said Sergeant Braithwaite in a tired voice. He was used to taking reports from Miss Hamilton-Smythe. He had a thick file of them he had compiled over several years, all of which were figments of her own imagination.

"He was tall, had black hair and a moustache. He was very aggressive and abusive towards me. Threatened to kill me. Thoroughly evil, I would say. Do you know he said he was also a serial killer?"

Sergeant Braithwaite raised his eyebrows in amused surprise. He thought the whole story highly unlikely.

"And where did this happen, Miss?"

"Behind the bushes at the top of the heath. Where the Vale of Health joins Squires Mount."

She drew herself up to her full height of five foot two and issued an imperious instruction to the desk sergeant.

"You must arrest him as soon as possible, Sergeant."

"We'll do our best, Miss."

"Oh, and another thing. He had a rifle."

It was the mention of a rifle that piqued his interest especially after the bombing the

Thursday before. Miss Hamilton-Smythe had never included weapons in her previous reports. Although he doubted there was anything in her allegations, he dispatched a young constable to have a look. Half an hour later he had him on the radio.

"Okay, sarge, I found the rifle. It's behind some bushes on the north-western edge of the heath. There's a suitcase with it. I don't want to touch anything just in case there are fingerprints. I reckon we need forensics up here."

Sergeant Braithwaite passed the message on to New Scotland Yard which sent a team to secure the area and retrieve the weapon. The news of the find hit the desk of superintendent McIntosh at seven o'clock that evening just as he was about to head home. He called his team together.

"Well, lads and lassies, it appears we may have a development in the Hampstead bombing case. A German sniper rifle and suitcase have been found in the bushes on Hampstead Heath just opposite Goloshin's house. The two things may or may not be connected but I'm working on the hypothesis that whoever planted the bomb might also have been trying to take a pot shot at Goloshin from the heath. If that is true, we're dealing with a very determined assassin. Forensics is checking to see whether there are any fingerprints on the rifle. If this is a professional, I doubt there will be but, Daniel, I want those results as soon as possible. In the meantime, we need to check on Goloshin's house. Anoushka, Brian, you come with me."

Hamish, Anoushka and police constable Brian Maxwell arrived in Hampstead within an hour to find Goloshin's house in darkness. They rang the intercom on the gate but there was no answer. The Goloshins may have gone but the housekeeper should still be there, thought Hamish. He suddenly had the uneasy feeling that something was wrong. He had that second sense that comes to policemen after decades of dealing with crime. He decided to force the gate open which triggered an alarm connected directly to the local police station. The three of them then approached the front door of the house. They rang the bell and knocked on the door. Again, no answer. They walked round to the back of the house. There were no lights on in any of the rooms. They came back to the front door as two squad cars arrived with blue lights flashing. Hamish went to show his warrant card and to explain what they were doing while Anoushka bent down to shine a pocket torch through the letterbox of the front door. She suddenly straightened up and shouted to her boss.

"Chief, you're not going to like this. I think there's a body in the hallway."

They left the crime scene an hour later having given statements to the local police who were searching the house and combing the surroundings for any evidence. The body had been provisionally identified from the driving licence in her handbag as a Mrs Anne Somerville, fifty-five years old, a resident of Finsbury Park. The medics had told Hamish that she had been stabbed twice in the heart and had probably died instantly.

On the way back in the squad car, Hamish reached a decision.

"Anoushka, I think your theory may be right. The bombing, the rifle and now the stabbing of the housekeeper. They're all connected with Goloshin. If that is so, then we're dealing with a very determined and dangerous man indeed. I want you to send out the photo of this man immediately to all police forces, airports, train stations and channel ferries saying that he is believed to be a certain David Mould and is wanted for questioning in relation to several incidents in the Hampstead area. We'd better warn them that he could be armed and that he might be travelling in disguise and under a false identity. I'll have to brief the commissioner first thing and I'll contact Goloshin and the local police in Spain. If we're right, this man may well be on his way to complete the job."

Hamish went to see the commissioner at ten the following morning having brought his whole team up to speed. He told him about the discovery of the sniper rifle, the murder of Goloshin's housekeeper and the theory that this was the work of a hitman, once a British soldier, who was now employed by the Russian secret service. The commissioner expressed his incredulity at this by raising his bushy eyebrows. He wondered for a moment whether the superintendent had lost the plot.

"Hamish, are you serious?"

"It was PC Khan's idea, and I must admit I was sceptical at first. However, sir, it fits the facts as far as we know them."

"Jesus Christ, as though we haven't got enough to worry about with the Russians."

"I'd like your permission, sir, to apply for a European arrest warrant. If our theory is correct, this man is already on his way to Spain to kill Ivan Goloshin."

"All right, Hamish but I hope you're right. We don't want to end up with egg on our faces."

He meant egg on his face, of course, thought Hamish.

"Of course not, sir. If I'm wrong, I'll carry the can."

Hamish stood up to go but paused at the door.

"By the way, sir. I'd also like to fly out to Spain to speak to Goloshin and liaise with the local police once the warrant is issued. I'd like to take PC Khan with me. It's her theory and she knows the case. I could also do with a second brain on this one."

"Okay, Hamish but for God's sake be diplomatic. We don't want any cock-up in international relations with either Spain or Russia."

Hamish left the commissioner's office with an air of determination. He was going to get this man, whoever he was. It was now just a question of time, and the clock was ticking.

CHAPTER 15 – Andalucia, Spain

They arrived early Monday evening in Malaga on the private jet. Yuri was already there with the car having taken an earlier commercial flight. Ivan's villa was an hour and a half away. It was located to the north-east of Frigiliana on one of the foothills that led up to the vast sierras of Tejeda, Almijara and Alhama. These were covered in scrubland and pine forests and pitted with deep ravines until you reached the snow-capped peak of the mountain of La Maroma from which you had a commanding view of the surrounding hills and the Mediterranean coast to the south.

It was a modest house by oligarch standards. Ivan had bought it on a whim in the early 1990s when he had just reached millionaire status. He had deliberately chosen a place far enough away from Malaga, where there were too many members of the Russian Mafia, and the seaside towns of the Costa del Sol, where there were too many tourists.

On the first floor there were five bedrooms each with an en-suite, two of which had balconies with views to the south over the valley of the river Chillar towards Nerja and the sea. The ground floor contained a garage and gym, the kitchen, four living rooms and three dining rooms, surrounded by a large terrace overlooking a garden and the valley below. A swimming pool was in the grounds together with two guesthouses, one of which was used by his bodyguards Boris and Yuri. Olive trees grew to the south and west of the house beyond which there were farms growing avocados and mangoes. In common with all the houses in the area, it was painted a blazing white which, in the heat of a Spanish summer, would illuminate all the hills down to the sea. To Ivan and Natasha, it had been an idyllic bolthole to which they could escape from the frenetic commercial and political life in St Petersburg.

As the car arrived in the driveway to the house, Ivan remembered the day they had first bought it, the joy on Natasha's face and the excited squeals from the twelve-year-old Irina when she jumped into the swimming pool. He felt a sudden stab of sadness to think that this had been one of the happiest days of his life. Now he was on the run, trying to escape an unknown FSB assassin. He hoped they were far enough away.

They climbed out of the car to be greeted by Pilar, the housekeeper and cook, and her husband José, who maintained the cars, the garden and pool. They were both about fifty years old and lived nearby where they owned an allotment growing vegetables which they sold to the local farm collective.

"Buenas tardes, Señor Ivan y Señorita Irina," said Pilar with a smile. Neither of them spoke English let alone Russian but over the years Ivan and Irina had come to learn enough Spanish to communicate.

"Buenas tardes, Pilar, it's lovely to see you again," said Ivan. "Let me introduce Peter, Irina's friend."

"Señor Peter, buenas tardes," said Pilar and added with a twinkle in her eye directed to Irina, "Muy guapo!" – a handsome boy. Irina giggled and gave her an affectionate kiss. Having known her since she was a young girl, Pilar was to her the aunt she never had.

Pilar had prepared her signature dish of paella which they ate with a robust Rioja wine outside on the terrace. It was a warm, balmy evening with no sound except the soft breeze through the olive trees below. After dinner Ivan and Peter sat together under a moonless sky and watched the stars which seemed to reflect the lights of the towns stretching to the coast. Out in the Mediterranean they could just see the dark smudges of container and cruise ships making their way to the port of Malaga. Ivan lit a cigar, poured himself a vodka and sighed contentedly.

"Is this your first time in Spain, Peter?"

"I went to Barcelona as a student once, but this is my first time in Andalucia. It's beautiful."

"Beautiful, yes, but there is also much blood in these hills. The Spaniards fought the Moors, had the Inquisition, exiled the Jews, and then fought each other during the Civil War.

There are caves around here where republicans hid from nationalists during the 1930s. So many people have died over the centuries, so many people killed. Reminds me of Russia."

By now Peter had got used to Ivan's philosophical musings. It was part of his character, he supposed, part of the melancholy that lay at the heart of the Russian soul. They sat in silence until Irina came out from the living room and broke the spell.

"Pilar tells me there is a fiesta this weekend in Nerja," she said excitedly. "We must go, Papa. I think we all need cheering up."

The prospect of a fiesta lightened the mood at least until the following morning when Ivan received three phone calls in rapid succession, all of which deepened his depression. The first was from superintendent McIntosh.

"Mr Goloshin. I'm sorry to be the bearer of sad news but I'm afraid your housekeeper in Hampstead was killed yesterday. A Mrs

Somerville, I believe. We think it is the same person who made the attempt on your life."

"Oh, my God! Why would anyone want to kill Anne?"

"It's likely that whoever it was wanted to find out where you might be. You need to be prepared for the worst scenario. We must assume that the threat is still real and that he knows where you are. We are making arrangements to issue a European arrest warrant and I shall contact your local guardia civil. My colleague and I will fly down this weekend to speak to them. In the meantime, I suggest you take extreme precautions."

An hour later the guardia civil at Nerja was on the phone.

"Señor Goloshin, this is inspector Gimenez. I wanted you to know that we have been contacted by the Metropolitan police in London concerning a potential threat to your life. If it is convenient, I should like to come and see you this afternoon to discuss security arrangements."

Pedro Gimenez was a young, recently promoted inspector who was more used to dealing with car thefts, robberies, and burglaries than possible assassination attempts on Russian oligarchs. Having dealt with many expatriates and tourists, however, his English was good, and he could not help but be excited at the responsibility of ensuring the safety of Mr Goloshin and possibly of apprehending the suspect who, from what the Met had told him, might be a hitman from the Russian secret services.

Ivan was understandably less enthusiastic about the involvement of the Spanish police. He just wanted a quiet life and had persuaded himself that the lights around the property and the video surveillance together with his bodyguards Boris and Yuri already provided enough security. But it would have been churlish to have refused the help of the Spanish police.

He could have done without the third and last call that morning.

"Hello, Ivan, old chap! It's John Amherst here." He gushed with overconfidence. "Look,

I'm awfully sorry to bother you but Matthew, your lawyer, told me you wouldn't mind. I'd just like to take you up on your kind offer to see me in Spain. If it's all right with you, I'd like to come out this Saturday evening. I shall have to fly back Sunday afternoon unfortunately, but this would give us time to discuss the loan we mentioned last year."

Ivan groaned inwardly and held the phone away while he muttered a series of Russian expletives which he was sure the Englishman would not understand. He managed to summon up enough patience to listen while Amherst told him again of his company's brilliant future and the need for a limited short-term loan. Amherst omitted to mention his impending bankruptcy and made no reference to the ongoing divorce proceedings which were likely to clear him out.

On the one hand Ivan had no real desire to see the man again. On the other he still thought it might be useful to have an ally in Parliament for his asylum claim if he ever decided to go back to England. After ten minutes of a rather one-sided conversation Ivan reluctantly agreed to the meeting, put the phone down in a state of exhaustion and poured himself a vodka. He was beginning to think that Spain was not far enough away from either England or Russia.

The police arrived after lunch. Pedro was accompanied by two other officers who toured the property with Boris and Yuri. They were broadly content with the security arrangements but agreed to provide an hourly drive by of a squad car just to make sure.

The next few days were spent in taking Peter around some of the main tourist sites in Andalucia. They drove up to Granada to the Alhambra, the vast red palace and fortress built by the Muslim emirs in what was then Al-Andalus and then visited the national parks in the Sierra Nevada. They had lunches in the local tavernas and strolled through the centres of Frigiliana and Nerja just like any other tourists except that either Boris or Yuri was never far behind.

On Saturday morning Boris drove them into Nerja for the Fiesta de las Cruces, the festival of the crosses, which takes place on 3 May every year. They felt the heat of the sun as they walked down the Calle Pintada, one of the roads that led to the central plaza of the old town and the Balcon de Europa, a promontory that looked over the Mediterranean.

While much of the Costa del Sol had been blighted by tall, concrete apartment blocks catering for tourists in search of sun, sea, and sangria, central Nerja still comprised many small two-storey cottages reflecting the nature of the fishing village it once was. For the fiesta, the sides of the narrow streets were filled with five foot tall gaily decorated crosses with brightly coloured bric-a-brac, plants, silks, and carpets while every tiny balcony was adorned with flowers. The town was bursting with throngs of people through which brass bands and wandering minstrels of every kind made their way with difficulty. In addition to the restaurants and cafés there were tapas bars and pop-up food stalls in every square and groups of señoras and señoritas processing in their finest polka dot dresses – red and black, green and white, yellow and blue. In the trees on the Balcon de Europa flocks of parakeets squawked loudly to be heard above the cacophony. Irina and

Peter smiled at each other as they pushed through the crowds. It was a far cry from either Hampstead or St Petersburg, but you could not fail to feel a sense of happy celebration.

They managed to find seats in one of the bars in the central Plaza Cavana near the church of El Salvador and ordered tapas and a bottle of Rioja for lunch. They gave money to a passing accordion player collecting for charity and to a trio of singers and a guitar player whose instrument was out of tune. They were singing the Elvis song Wooden Heart in a strong Spanish accent. To Peter it all seemed so gloriously disorganised and joyful. Even Ivan, depressed as he was, began to smile and laugh.

In the melee of people, they did not notice the man hiding in the corner of the plaza who was watching their every move. Neither did Boris who had taken a seat in a café nearby and was sipping a soda water. This man in the corner did not laugh. Nor did he smile. He was just waiting patiently. He would continue to follow them until the time was right.

They returned to the villa at six that evening to find that Amherst had already arrived from Malaga and had made himself at home with a glass of wine on the terrace.

"Ah, Ivan, old boy. Good to see you. Hope you don't mind. Your housekeeper offered me a drink."

"Of course not, Mr Amherst. What do they say in Spanish? Mi casa es su casa."

"John, please" said Amherst as he took another swig of wine. The obvious insincerity of Goloshin's welcome passed him by completely.

Ivan smiled wryly and introduced Irina and Peter. They agreed to defer discussion of the loan until the following morning. In fact, Ivan did not want to discuss the issue at all and had already decided not to lend any money to this man whose honesty, he had concluded, was at best doubtful. He was angry with himself at ever having extended an invitation to him but at least the unwelcome guest would be departing the following day.

They had an uneasy supper together during which Amherst got progressively drunker and more flirtatious with Irina. Peter decided the man was thoroughly obnoxious. Finally, around ten o'clock, they all went to bed early, and the house fell silent.

As the house went dark, a shadowy figure appeared in the olive trees in the valley below. It was a warm night, and the air was calm. Apart from the distant rumble of the revels of the fiesta on the coast, all was quiet. Nothing moved and nothing could be seen except from time to time a reflection of starlight on the binoculars which were trained on the windows of the villa.

CHAPTER 16 – Andalucia, Spain

After the events in Hampstead David Mould had returned to the hotel in Cricklewood to collect his things and then made his way to Stansted where he booked a cheap flight to Malaga using his passport as Martin Hauptmann. On the way he made a call to Hans in Germany – he was running out of money, and he would need supplies in Spain. Hans was curt on the phone once he had told him what he needed.

"You need to get this done, Martin. I will make the arrangements, but this is the last time, you understand. Either Goloshin dies or you need not come back."

David swore under his breath as he told Hans what he needed and took down the address of the contact in Malaga. This mission had now become existential. He had to succeed, or risk being cast into a stateless limbo being unable to return to either England or Germany. The UK police would eventually find him in the first case and his former friends would undoubtedly eliminate him in the second.

He had been lucky so far. There was no increased police presence at the airport and so he assumed that there was no extended manhunt for the killer of Goloshin's housekeeper. In any event, he reasoned, there was no way of linking Martin Hauptmann with either the bombing or the murder. And who was Martin Hauptmann anyway? He could as well be his alias, Eberhard Wagner. Or even his real identity, David Mould. No one would be able to identify him as a suspect, unless that batty old lady with the schnauzer had reported him to the police and they somehow had made connections. He discounted that idea as fanciful. Surely no one would believe her. And he had killed the only other person who could have identified him. He was truly sorry about the housekeeper, of course, but it had to be done. It was too risky to leave her alive. By the time he had cleared customs in Malaga he had rationalised any fears he might have had and regained his confidence. No one was after him and no one could find him.

He took a taxi from the airport to a dingy bed-and-breakfast in the port area where he booked in for the night. In the morning he went in search of Hans' contact. He found him in a dirty container parked near the docks with a hand-painted sign on the side – St Petersburg Logistics Inc. He knocked on the door and went in to be greeted by a burly, long-haired man in a soiled vest with bushy eyebrows and a beard who identified himself as Vassily and looked at him with immediate suspicion. David was not surprised to find a Russian. The FSB had always worked in close but not always friendly harmony with the Russian mafia and the criminal fraternity of St Petersburg as well as those from Italy and the UK had long colonised the Costa del Sol. So much so that it had earned the English epithet, probably coined by some grizzled Metropolitan police officer, of the Costa del Crime.

"Hans sent me. You have something for me?" asked David looking the Russian in the eye.

"Are you Martin?"

David showed his passport at which the Russian opened a drawer in his desk and took out two packages. The first contained ten thousand euros while the second held a PSS silent pistol, a standard issue for Soviet special forces and secret police. The man handed over the package with the money but kept the pistol.

"If you want the pistol complete with holster and cartridges, it'll be an extra two thousand."

"I thought Hans had taken care of everything."

David spoke slowly and calmly. The additional payment had never been part of the deal, but it was not worth an argument since the man was just as likely to use the pistol to shoot him and pocket the whole of the cash. It would be easy then to dump the body in the sea and claim that Martin Hauptmann never turned up. He paid the man his money and left.

He went to a large, local hypermarket and purchased a backpack, black jumper, balaclava, and gloves together with hiking boots and jacket, a pair of trainers, binoculars, and a pocket torch. He knew roughly where Goloshin's villa lay since he had visited Frigiliana before on one of his previous missions and suspected he would need to access it through the countryside. At a bookshop in town, he bought a detailed map of the Costa del Sol showing hiking paths. He then hired a car for which he paid cash and drove along the coastal road to Nerja where he found a cheap student hostel to the north of the town about five miles from Frigiliana.

The next day he got up early and drove up to see precisely where Goloshin's villa was located. It lay on a hill isolated from the town overlooking olive groves and the valley down to Nerja. Access was by a rough road that was little more than a dirt track. He could see it was surrounded by a low wall no more than five foot high and had a large terrace on the ground floor and balconies on the first. He had already decided that this was not a job for a sniper rifle. He needed to make sure this time and a handgun was the only option.

At midday he returned to the hotel and, after a light lunch, put on his hiking gear and walked down a track behind the hostel which led to the Rio Chillar. The riverbed was designated as a hiking path since it was dry was most of the year. It provided a rocky trail leading up to the olive groves on the hillside just below the villa. He met one other hiker on the way but otherwise the area was deserted. Any Spanish observer would simply have assumed he was just another mad foreign tourist out for a walk. It was hot in the early afternoon and by the time he reached the trees he was sweating profusely. He sat down in the shade of the trees and took a swig from a bottle of water in his backpack. It had taken an hour, but he was now just fifty yards away from the rear of the villa. It would take more time at night but after exercises on Salisbury plain and Germany he was used to that.

Crouched down behind the olive trees, he surveyed the villa with his binoculars. There appeared to be lights on all four corners of the wall enclosing the property. He assumed there was also video surveillance somewhere, but he was prepared to take the risk of being caught on camera since he had no intention of spending a long time completing the hit. He watched as a large, solidly built man exited one of the other two houses on the property and walk slowly around the swimming pool. It was the same bodyguard he had seen in Hampstead. He would be collateral damage if necessary. On the first floor he could see two large French windows opening onto an extensive balcony. These must be bedrooms, he concluded. That's where it would have to be done, at night while they were asleep.

The next night he left the hostel at two in the morning and retraced his steps in the dark up the trail on the riverbed to the vantage point in the olive grove. An hour and a half. Upon his return he was satisfied that the whole operation could be completed within four hours. Over breakfast that morning he learned from the proprietor of the hostel that there was to be a fiesta in Nerja that weekend. An ideal time since the police would be occupied day and night with drunken tourists. He just had to be sure that Goloshin was staying at the villa.

On Saturday morning he drove up again to the house and parked near the front gates far enough away not to be conspicuous but near enough to see the exits and entrances. After half an hour he was pleased to see Goloshin and a young couple get into a car and be driven away by the bodyguard. He followed at a discreet distance and entered the central municipal car park of Nerja just behind them. He heard them laughing together as he walked behind them into the centre of town to join the crowds attending the festivities. He watched them sit down and take lunch in a plaza and, for a moment or two, wondered whether he also might one day be happy like them. He doubted he would be so lucky.

He left the hostel for the last time at two o'clock that Sunday morning. He wore his hiking boots and had everything necessary in his backpack. He could still hear the noises of the fiesta in the town but these receded as he walked up the trail once more to Goloshin's villa. It was another warm night, but he made good progress as the path was illuminated by the pale light of a new moon. He arrived at the olive grove in under an hour. He waited, watched, and listened. There were no sounds and no movements around the villa and all the lights were off in the house. He exchanged his hiking boots for trainers, pulled on his black balaclava and fitted the silencer onto the gun and put it back in the holster. It was time.

It took him just minutes to cover the open ground and clamber over the wall. He dropped silently to the ground and waited for a moment. Again, no sounds. He walked quickly to the corner of the house and climbed up the edge of the wall until he could grab the parapet and roll over onto the balcony. He could see that the sets of French windows for both bedrooms had been left ajar to let in the night air. He took out the gun. Without a noise he gently prised open the first window and pulled the net curtains apart. In the dark he could just make out a large bed on which two people were asleep. They must be the young couple he had seen. He moved quickly onto the next window and did the same. On the bed was one figure. It had to be Goloshin. He took aim at the head and fired three shots in quick succession. They made little more noise than cans of soda being opened. The body made no sound but jerked once or twice and then stopped moving.

Immediately he ran back to the edge of the parapet and jumped down into the garden below. He suddenly heard a noise behind him and assumed it was the bodyguard on guard duty. He turned and fired. He heard the man grunt and fall to the ground but had no time to look. The adrenaline pumping, he ran to the wall and vaulted over. Another minute and he was grabbing his backpack and running through the olive trees and scrubland down the trail back to Nerja. Behind him he thought he heard shouts and a piercing scream and imagined that an alarm had already been sent to the police. He tried to increase the pace but had to be careful not to fall over the rocks that were strewn over the path. He did not dare draw attention to himself by turning on the torchlight. It was consequently harder work going down than coming up and he recognised he was no longer the young soldier he once was.

Gradually he slowed down as he realised that he could hear no police sirens on the main road on the hill above which led down to Nerja from Frigiliana. The fiesta was over, and the night was eerily quiet. Perhaps the shouts had nothing to do with the shooting, he thought. Perhaps there was no alarm. Half an hour later, however, he suddenly saw lights moving in the darkness of the valley below and was seized with a panic. There were torches coming up the hill towards him and following the same trail that he was on. Had the police already organised a manhunt? He knew he could not afford to be found. Whoever it was might ask some difficult questions. He had to get off the main track. He was not to know that it was simply a group of Norwegian hillwalkers determined to get an early start on a day's excursion.

He knew from the map he had studied that the dry riverbed of the Rio Chillar had many tributary paths to the left and right which led back into the hills. He took the first he came to. It wound upwards to the left and grew steeper as he climbed. After twenty minutes he finally arrived breathless at a large opening in the rock face on the side of the hill. It was the entrance to a cave. It would provide him with a safe place to hide and recuperate at least until mid-morning when he could then make his way back down to the town. He turned on the torchlight. While the air outside was cooling with a breeze veering to the north, it was warm inside the cave.

David knew of the famous Cuevas de Nerja, vast cathedral like caverns extending kilometres under the surrounding hills and formed millions of years ago by water dissolving the marble rock and creating giant stalagmites and stalactites. He was also aware that the foothills in the surrounding area were dotted with hundreds of other caves which had been used for millennia. Some had provided hideouts for the Republicans during the latter stages of the Spanish Civil War as they were hunted down by Franco's troops. Perhaps this had been one of them, he thought as he penetrated deeper into the darkness. Certainly, the floor seemed to have been worn down by generations of footsteps.

He stopped about hundred yards in and sat down with his backpack against the wall of the cave which he now realised was much bigger than he originally thought. He suddenly felt exhausted but pleased that he had accomplished his mission. He hoped to God that he could now retire and that his masters in Moscow would let him go. His eyelids drooped and within a few minutes he was fast asleep.

David had not seen the sign which had fallen to the floor on the other side of the cave – PELIGRO EXTREMO - RIESGOS DE CAIDA DE ROCAS – extreme danger, risk of rockfalls. Nor did he hear the occasional drip of water from the roof of the cave which had taken thousands of years to form the large stalactite above his head.

It was twenty past seven and the sun was beginning to rise over the hills of the Sierra Nevada. A pale light was filtering slowly into the cave. There was a faint sound of small, scurrying animals and the occasional high-pitched muttering of a bat. David was still fast asleep, so he did not hear the sharp cracking above him. Suddenly there was a roar as a ton of rock above tore itself from the roof of the cave and smashed onto David's body. He was obliterated in an instant. The sound of the rockfall reverberated in the recesses of the caverns in the hill. Where David had once been sleeping nothing could be seen but rock and dust and the shattered remnants of the stalactite. The body would never be found. The water would continue to drip from the roof of the cave over hundreds of years gradually dissolving the clothing and flesh and bleaching the bones. Eventually there would be another stalagtite pointing down to the grave. The dice had been thrown and David had been unlucky.

CHAPTER 17

It was just after eight on Sunday morning when Inspector Pedro Gimenez received a call from a guardia civil squad car. He had been on night duty for the fiesta in Nerja and was looking forward to going back home for a few hours before the arrival of superintendent McIntosh and his associate who were due to arrive from London at midday. The night had seen nothing but minor disturbances and a bar fight between an Irishman and a Swede in the centre of Nerja. A drunken argument about who was the better football club – Manchester United or Manchester City, neither of which team they supported. The last thing he was expecting was that a murder had been committed on his watch.

He was told on the phone that a shooting had taken place at the villa Goloshin in Frigiliana. A squad car had been conducting a regular patrol of the house and had been stopped by a distraught young man. There was one fatality and one man who had been shot in the leg. An ambulance had been called but an inspector was needed to take over the investigation. For a moment he thought about leaving it to his deputy who was due to take over the day shift, but it was he who had overseen the security arrangements for Goloshin, and he remained responsible. He phoned his wife Maria to tell her he would be late.

He arrived at the Goloshin villa to find two ambulances parked outside and several police officers scouring the grounds. In one of the ambulances medics were treating a young man for a wound in the leg. A bullet had passed straight through the muscle, but he would make a rapid recovery and did not need hospital treatment. The officer who had phoned told him that the fatality was a Mr Goloshin and that the body was upstairs in one of the bedrooms. Pedro entered the house to find Irina and Peter sitting on a sofa in one of the living rooms. She was sobbing quietly while he was trying to comfort her as best he could.

"Señorita Irina, Señor Peter. I'm so sorry to hear of your loss."

"They finally got him. Those bastards shot him while he was asleep. He had no chance. They killed my father."

Irina sobbed again and wiped her eyes with a handkerchief. Pedro paused for a moment to let her compose herself.

"Can you tell me exactly what happened?"

Peter looked at the inspector and took up the story.

"I suppose it was about seven o'clock this morning. It was still dark. Irina and I were in the bedroom next to her father's. Suddenly we heard a shout from the garden and ran out onto the balcony. Down below we could see Yuri holding his leg and groaning. He told us to check the house. I went into Ivan's bedroom to find the body on the bed. It was obvious that he had been shot several times. There was blood everywhere. I immediately phoned 112 for the police and then went outside to wait for them by the gate. Shortly afterwards I flagged down a passing squad car and told them what had happened."

At that moment Boris appeared at the living room door and nodded to Peter and Irina.

"This is Boris, inspector, the other security guard," said Peter. "He left the house before everything happened. He had to take an overnight guest to Malaga airport for an early flight. It's a British MP and he had to get back to London for an important meeting."

"I shall need his details just in case we have to interview him."

"Of course, inspector."

"And did any of you see anyone else? Is there anyone else in the house?"

"Pilar and José, the housekeeper and her husband, live off the property and were not here. The only one who saw anything was Yuri. There is video surveillance, but we have not had time to look at it."

"You must catch whoever did this, inspector," said Irina.

"We shall do our best, señorita."

Pedro went outside and spoke to Yuri who could only report a fleeting figure dressed in black with a balaclava who had leapt over the garden wall and disappeared into the olive groves below. Not a lot to go on, thought Pedro as he went upstairs to the bedroom to see the body. A forensics officer was already there taking photographs and looking for bullets and fingerprints although, as far as the latter were concerned, Pedro doubted that he would find any of the perpetrator.

The body itself lay on white sheets which had been soaked with blood from the wounds to the head which was now little more than a mangled piece of flesh and bone from which no features could be distinguished. Pedro thought for a moment as he contemplated the crime scene and then returned to the living room.

"Señorita Irina, I take it you can confirm that the body upstairs is, indeed, that of your father Ivan Goloshin?"

"Of course, inspector. Who else would it be? It was my father who was hunted down and slaughtered by the Russian secret services, God damn them."

"Very well. There will have to be an autopsy, of course, and we shall need formal statements from all of you as soon as you feel able to come to the police station. I should like to take the videotape if I may."

Irina nodded and then added, "There's one thing, inspector. I don't want my father to stay like that. It's horrible. I should like him to be cremated as soon as possible. Within a week at most That's what he would have wanted. So, I should be grateful if you could expedite the autopsy."

"I'm sure I can make that happen. Again, my condolences, señorita."

Having ensured that two policemen would remain guarding the villa, Pedro returned to the office in Nerja to find the European arrest warrant for a man suspected of a bombing in Hampstead, the attempted assassination of Ivan Goloshin and the murder of his housekeeper. Superintendent McIntosh had already told him to expect it. It had been delayed by over five days owing to the vagueness of the description but had now been forwarded to all the main police forces along the Costa del Sol. He looked at the photo and wondered how useful it would be now. If this was, indeed, the professional hitman they suspected, it was already too late.

He gave orders to set up a roadblock on the main road from Frigiliana to Nerja and to send officers out to comb the area around Goloshin's villa. It was now almost ten o'clock. If the time of the murder was correct, the suspect already had a three hour start on them – enough time to get to Algeciras and board a ferry to Ceuta in North Africa or even Tarifa to Tangiers. The likelihood of him ever being caught was receding by the minute.

Superintendent McIntosh and PC Khan arrived at the police station at eleven thirty having taken an early flight from Stansted and hired a car in Malaga.

"Inspector Gimenez, it's good of you to see us," said Hamish.

"Call me Pedro, please."

"Well, my name is Hamish, and this is Anoushka."

"You're not going to like what I have to tell you, Hamish."

"Where have I heard that before?" said Hamish giving Anoushka a wry smile.

"Ivan Goloshin was shot dead early this morning in his villa. According to his daughter and her boyfriend, the attack took place at about seven o'clock. His daughter has confirmed the identity of the body. It seems likely that the perpetrator is the same man you're after although, of course, we can't be sure."

"Jesus, we're too late then." Hamish paled visibly at the news. He had failed in his duty to protect.

"We should get the autopsy report in a day or two. We have a videotape of the attack if you want to see it, but I doubt it will be useful."

They watched the tape together. The camera covered the whole of the rear of the villa including the first-floor balconies, the garden, and the swimming pool. The film showed a man dressed in black and wearing a balaclava walking up to the balcony. For a brief time, he was out of view and then three cracks were heard. The man reappeared seconds later running to the rear of the garden. Another man, Yuri the bodyguard, came into the frame with a shout but then fell with another sound of a pistol crack by which time the man in the balaclava had disappeared over the wall. The whole attack lasted little more than a few minutes.

"As you can see, Hamish, there is very little to identify the man."

"I'm sorry, sir, I thought you told us the attack took place at seven o'clock," said Anoushka thoughtfully. "The tape shows that the attack began at 0312 and ended at 0320."

"I expect the daughter and her boyfriend were just confused," said Pedro. "I think that's understandable, don't you?"

"I suppose so." Anoushka was unconvinced but let it go.

"Well, if you'll excuse me, I must now prepare a briefing for the press conference this afternoon in Malaga. Of course, you are welcome to come."

By the time the press had gathered at the main police headquarters in Malaga that afternoon, the news of the murder of a Russian businessman on the Costa del Sol had already spread far and wide. Goloshin might not have been in the big league of oligarchs, but his assassination would still make the headlines. In addition to stringers from the Spanish national papers, there were reporters from the major European outlets and cameras from the main TV stations. The police statement kept to the facts such as they were and asked for privacy for the family during this difficult time. There were the usual speculative questions as to who might be responsible – the Mafia, the Camorra, gangsters from St Petersburg, secret services of a foreign state – but these were easily deflected. Investigations were ongoing.

Returning to the hotel in Nerja that evening, Hamish and Anoushka were both dispirited. They had failed to catch the man while he was still in London, Hamish thought, and he felt the failure keenly. He was now convinced that the Russian secret services were behind it. Only they would have had the single-minded determination to hunt the man down from one country to another until they succeeded.

From the bar in the hotel where they were having a consolation whiskey, Hamish phoned the commissioner in London to give him an update on the investigation. He could hear the relief in Sir Robert Lowell's voice.

"Well, Hamish, at least it's no longer our problem. I'm sorry for his family, of course, but after all he was not a British citizen, and we must now leave it to the Spanish authorities. I expect you'll be coming back soon to deal with the other important cases on your desk."

"God almighty, Anoushka, that man is such a shit," said Hamish as he put the phone down.

"He's right, of course, boss. We did our best. It just wasn't enough."

"We'll go and see the daughter tomorrow morning and then wait for the autopsy report. Meanwhile, as we're now definitively off duty let's have another whiskey."

At around ten the following morning they drove up to the Goloshin villa and presented their condolences to Irina. On the way back in the car, Hamish was reflective.

"Did you not think she was remarkably……, what's the word? Collected, I suppose. I mean, considering she'd just lost her father, her only living relative, in a violent attack, I expected her to be more upset."

"Grief affects people differently, boss."

"I'm sure you're right, Anoushka. I'm just getting too suspicious in my old age."

Anoushka was still bothered by the discrepancy between the timing on the videotape and the reported time of the attack.

"I'm still wondering why it took them four hours after the shooting to phone the police. Seems an awfully long time."

"I expect they were trying to get over the shock," said Hamish. "To quote our esteemed commissioner, it is no longer our problem."

CHAPTER 18

Having taken formal statements from everyone in the villa on the Tuesday afternoon, inspector Gimenez received the autopsy report on Goloshin first thing Wednesday morning and translated the gist of the conclusions to Hamish and Anoushka in his office.

"The body is that of a white male approximately fifty years old in reasonably good condition. The indications are that death probably took place between three and eight am on 4 May 2002 and was caused by three bullets all of which penetrated the back of his head and exited through the frontal lobe causing extensive injury to facial tissue. There was massive trauma to the cranial cavities and the brain and considerable blood loss. There is little doubt that the victim died instantaneously. All the bullets were retrieved at the crime scene, and all were heavy calibre indicating that they were probably fired at close range by a gun fitted with a silencer – possibly a PSS as used by the KGB Spetsnaz or an MSP Groza silent pistol. Both types of guns have been commonly used in assassinations."

"So, it was the Russians?" said Hamish.

"It's impossible to say," said Pedro. "Such guns can be bought by criminals on the black market so it could be anyone. For the right price, you can pick them up easily in Malaga if you know the right person. In any case the Russians have specifically denied any responsibility."

"Any news on your search for the gunman?"

"None at all. There is now a Europewide manhunt underway, but I must tell you, Hamish, that in my opinion if this was a professional assassination then whoever is responsible, has now disappeared. Just like that – how do you say in English 'una bocanada de humo' - a puff of smoke, no?" Pedro clicked his fingers philosophically and smiled with an air of resignation.

Waiting for their flight back to London, Hamish bought the Times and the Guardian in the airport lounge. The story of Goloshin's death was now relegated to the inner pages and would soon disappear altogether and become a cold case never to be resolved. You win some, you lose some, he thought philosophically. He still could not avoid feeling despondent that he had not been able to prevent the murder of the oligarch. Then he brightened up at the thought that he would nevertheless recommend Anoushka for promotion. Her theory might not have been proved but he knew in his gut that she was right.

Back in London the director MI5 had also followed the story in the newspapers and been briefed on the case. As far as he was concerned, it was one less oligarch to worry about. For a moment he thought about that chap in Greenwood's department who was involved with Goloshin's daughter and had decided to resign from the service. What was his name? Peter Johnson. He hoped he was happy with the decision he had made.

In Russia, the shooting of Goloshin was only mentioned in a few publications and did not even reach the television news. A brief statement was issued from the Kremlin repudiating any spurious allegations in the Western press that it was in any way to blame. Behind the red walls of the fortress, however, there were smiles in certain offices that one more critic of the regime had disappeared forever. There would, of course, be others.

Inspector Gimenez kept his promise to Irina and released the body for cremation which she had arranged to take place at 3 pm the following Saturday at the nearest crematorium in Almuñecar some 25 minutes up the coast. They managed to find an Orthodox priest to conduct a brief service. Ivan Goloshin was not a believer, but Irina considered it only appropriate. There were only Irina, Peter, Boris and Matthew, Ivan's lawyer, present in the chapel as the coffin slid slowly away through the curtains to the music of Rachmaninov's Vespers.

As they came out of the chapel Irina dabbed her eyes with a handkerchief. She looked beautiful, thought Peter, in a black dress and veil which contrasted vividly with the blazing sunlight and the brilliant blue sky.

Inspector Gimenez was waiting for them at the entrance.

"Señorita Irina, allow me to express my condolences once again."

"Thank you, Inspector, it was kind of you to come."

"I expect you'll be flying back to England now."

"No, Inspector. We shall be going to my father's property in Argentina. There are now too many sad memories for me both in London and here in Spain."

"I understand, señorita." There was an awkward silence while the inspector wondered what he could say next.

"We haven't given up, you know. We still hope to catch the killer."

He hoped that the lie would be some consolation but they both knew the truth. Irina nodded and shook his hand.

They collected the ashes first thing the following Monday morning on the way to the airport. They were in a simple plastic urn accompanied by the death certificate. Irina got Boris to stop the car in Benalmadena and she walked down with Peter hand in hand to the beach. There were few people around. The sun seeking tourists had not yet come out to play. She knelt by the surf and carefully poured the ashes into the sea saying a few words she did so. They watched for a moment in silence as the waves lapped back-and-forth. On the way back to the car she placed the urn in a rubbish bin but kept the death certificate. At last, it was over.

They had booked first-class tickets on a KLM flight to Buenos Aires which would not arrive until early the following morning. As they settled into their seats on the connecting flight in Amsterdam and sipped champagne, Irina kissed Peter and smiled radiantly. She was happy for the first time in many months. Boris was on a seat behind them looking at the menu. He too smiled contentedly. As they took off Peter looked through the Times that he had bought at the airport. He read the article on page three.

"Police have reported the disappearance of the backbench MP John Amherst. He was last seen on Saturday 3 May when he took a flight to Malaga for unknown reasons. He was due back the following day but did not take the return flight and has not been seen since. His wallet and passport were found at the airport. His wife, Helena Amherst, has expressed extreme concern about his whereabouts. Speculations are rife that his disappearance may have something to do with his current acrimonious divorce proceedings and the financial difficulties of his firm, Amherst Construction Ltd, which has recently been placed in receivership."

They arrived in Buenos Aires at 9 o'clock the following morning. While Boris attended to the luggage, Irina and Peter went into the first-class airport lounge.

He was already there drinking coffee. He had taken a taxi from his ranch outside the city in the early hours to be sure that he was here on time. Irina ran towards him and enveloped him in a delighted embrace, laughing and crying at the same time.

"My dear papa, you cannot know how happy I am to see you."

"My darling daughter, not as happy as I am!"

Ivan clasped Peter in a bear hug and kissed him on both cheeks. They then sat down and ordered champagne.

"тост за будущее! – A toast to the future!" said Ivan as they clinked glasses. "Everything went well then?"

"Everything went according to plan." said Irina. "Thanks to Peter."

"You acted the part of the grieving daughter beautifully, Olga," said Peter. "Perhaps you should go on stage."

"Why, thank you, Lensky. And I'm glad you were not shot."

Irina laughed as she gave Peter an affectionate kiss.

"And Amherst?" said Ivan.

"I'm truly sorry about John Amherst," said Peter, "but it was the only way, Ivan, that you were ever going to get out of the ever-present threat of assassination. And he was dead anyway. Who was to know that Amherst would be there and that the assassin, whoever he is, would kill him instead of you."

"бросок костей – a roll of the dice," said Ivan reflectively.

"It took some time to make sure there was nothing to identify the body," continued Peter. "Boris left his wallet and passport at the airport when he dropped you off for your flight and got rid of his other belongings on the way back. They are looking for him now but, of course, they won't find him. His ashes are in the Mediterranean. Thanks to him you are now officially dead, and we have the certificate to prove it."

"What about Yuri?" asked Ivan.

"Yuri has been handsomely recompensed and has gone back to Russia. He knows nothing."

Boris appeared with the luggage and gave his boss a bear hug as he beamed with happiness.

"Boris Ivanovich, I thank you from the bottom of my heart." said Ivan proffering him a glass of champagne.

"You all know that this will be a new life and that there is no going back?"

"I know, papa, but we are together and that's what mama would have wanted. That's all that counts."

"You'll have to get used to calling me Vladimir," said Ivan cheerfully wafting his false passport in the name of Vladimir Fyodorovich Stepanov.

"I'm not sure that mama would have approved of your first name." Irina looked at his father sternly then burst out into giggles. She took Peter's hand and kissed it.

"My darling Natasha, if only she was here," said Ivan sadly and then smiled at the assembled company. "Мои дорогие, пойдем домой! My dears, let's go home."